LET'S-TALK-ABOUT-IT STORIES FOR KIDS

Secrets of the Best Choice

LOIS WALFRID JOHNSON

Illustrations by Virginia Peck

NAVPRESS
A MINISTRY OF THE NAVIGATORS
P.O. BOX 35001, COLORADO SPRINGS, COLORADO 80935

The Navigators is an international Christian
organization. Jesus Christ gave His follow-
ers the Great Commission to go and make
disciples (Matthew 28:19). The aim of The
Navigators is to help fulfill that commission by
multiplying laborers for Christ in every nation.

NavPress is the publishing ministry of The
Navigators. NavPress publications are tools
to help Christians grow. Although publications alone cannot make disciples or change
lives, they can help believers learn biblical
discipleship, and apply what they learn to their
lives and ministries.

Third printing, 1991

With the exception of "A Look in the Mirror,"
which is based on a true incident, the stories
and characters in this book are fictitious. Any
resemblance to actual persons, living or dead,
is coincidental.

Unless otherwise identified, Scripture quota-
tions are from the *Holy Bible: New International
Version* (NIV). Copyright © 1973, 1978, 1984,
International Bible Society. Used by permission
of Zondervan Bible Publishers. Other versions
used are the *Good News Bible* (GNB), copyright
© American Bible Society 1976; *The Living
Bible* (TLB), copyright 1971 by Tyndale House
Publishers, Wheaton, Illinois, used by permission; and The *New American Standard Bible*
(NASB), © The Lockman Foundation, 1960,
1962, 1963, 1968, 1971, 1972, 1973, 1975,
and 1977.

Printed in the United States of America

CONTENTS

To all the Sventeks—
Linda and Steve
Sarah, Rachel, Anna,
Sam, Joel, Stacey, and Andrew—
because I love you.

AUTHOR

When Lois Walfrid Johnson was nine years old she wondered, "What do I want to be when I grow up?" She sensed God's call to be a writer. If she could possibly write a book, she wanted to tell others what she believed about Jesus Christ.

That desire stayed with her through high school, college, and the early years of her marriage to Roy Johnson, an elementary school teacher. When the youngest of their three children entered first grade, Lois became a full-time free-lance writer. Her articles, poetry, and books have been published in English-speaking countries throughout the world and translated into nine languages.

Lois Johnson is the author of thirteen books,

including *You're Worth More Than You Think!*, *Thanks for Being My Friend*, and *You Are Wonderfully Made!* in the LET'S-TALK-ABOUT-IT series. She has also written *Just a Minute, Lord* and *You're My Best Friend, Lord* for pre-teens; *Come as You Are* for young teens; *Gift in My Arms, Either Way, I Win*, and *Falling Apart or Coming Together* for adults. Lois leads seminars and retreats and speaks at churches and conferences throughout the United States.

ACKNOWLEDGMENTS

My warm thanks to these people: Charette Kvernstoen, Traci Mullins, and Kathy Yanni for their encouragement and support; Jeffrey Johnson, Kevin Johnson, Lois Carlson, Jeff Boyum, Laurie Merritt, and my critique group for help with the manuscript; my husband, Roy, for being God's special gift as I make what I believe to be God's choices.

TO KIDS WHO READ THIS BOOK

Ooops! Company's coming! Your room looks like a tornado hit, and you have just twenty minutes to clean.

Well, only one thing to do. Take the dirty socks, the gym shoes, the balls, the books, the crumpled blouse or shirt, the twice-worn jeans. Shove them under the bed. Then put on a happy face. Smile. To all outward appearances, you have a clean room.

All of us have times when we'd like to hide another kind of dirty socks. If you're like the rest of us, you probably know how it feels. You want to take everything you're thinking and feeling and push it under the bed. Isn't it easier to ignore whatever you don't like? To pretend it's not there?

11

Yet the pressure builds up. You not only have a messy hidden place. You also have so many feelings scrunched down inside you're like a balloon ready to burst.

There's another way. Talking about what bothers you. Getting things out in the open. Connecting with that right person who listens and lets you talk. That person will understand how you feel and build you up, rather than tear you down.

If you don't know someone like that, ask God for a person who loves you as He does—just the way you are. Maybe it will be a mom or dad, a grandparent, uncle, or aunt. Perhaps a neighbor, teacher, pastor, or just someone you think is great.

When you find that person, start talking. Bring things out from under the bed. You'll find that something special happens. Not every problem is suddenly solved, but the right person helps you see your situation from a different angle. You pick up new ideas on how to handle something. Instead of feeling all alone, you know you have someone who wants the best for you. You become a happier person.

In each of the stories that follow, kids face problems like yours or like those of your friends. As you think about the stories, you'll discover that sometimes these kids need to choose between right and wrong. On other occasions, between good and better. Put yourself in their place. Ask yourself, "What would I do if this were happening to me or to one of my friends?" When you think about the questions at the end of each story, you'll see new ways of making choices—of dealing with those things that bother you.

Then turn the book upside down to read the Bible verse that's given. Repeat the verse to yourself until you receive the encouragement you need. Read the prayer, or pray one of your own. Whenever you turn to God, you receive a power greater than your own.

As you begin to read, ask Jesus to help you in the adventure of learning to talk about things that are important to you—the adventure in which you discover *secrets of the best choice.*

ARE YOU A QUITTER?

For three days Stacey had looked forward to this moment. Standing on the corral fence, she watched as her friend Joel slipped a bridle over his pony's head.

"Reggie's a good pony," he said. "I've been riding him for three years."

Stacey glanced at two larger horses drinking water at a trough. They seemed so high that she was glad to start out on a pony. Yet she felt sure she could handle any horse well.

"I'll give you a lift," said Joel. Stacey put one foot in his clasped hands, and swung up over Reggie's bare back. "Lay your rein on the right side of his neck, and he'll turn left. Lay it on the left side, and he'll go right."

Moments later Stacey was off. As she and Reggie started down the drive, she felt excited, then sure of herself. "I knew I could handle it," she thought.

Soon they reached the place where the road edged around the pasture fence. Just as Stacey rounded the corner, the other horses in the corral ran straight for the fence. Without warning, Reggie plunged away from them. As he went right, Stacey went left. With a jolt she landed in the middle of the road.

"Ouch!" she groaned. Too stunned to move, she felt shaken in every bone of her body.

"Are you okay?" called Joel, running to help.

"Dumb horse," answered Stacey. "I won't try that again."

But Joel had a different idea. "You need to get back on."

"Are you kidding?" asked Stacey.

"You don't have to be afraid," said Joel. "He's never thrown me. He was frightened by the horses coming at him."

"But Reggie's your pony. He likes you."

"Are you a quitter?" asked Joel. "If you don't get back on now you'll be too afraid to try again. Besides, Reggie has to know you're boss, or he'll think he can get by with throwing people."

Stacey thought it through. "Welllll—maybe you're right. The longer I think about it, the more scared I get." Slowly she stood up.

17

Joel led Reggie over to a stump. "This time I'll ride with you. You first. I'll hold him."

A moment later they were off. Soon Stacey's fear disappeared, as happiness welled up within her. After awhile, Joel slid off.

By the end of the afternoon Stacey felt like a seasoned rider. "What if I had missed this?" she asked herself. "What if I hadn't tried again?"

TO TALK ABOUT

▶What do you especially like to do?

▶Were you good at it the first time you tried, or did you have to make a choice the way Stacey did?

▶If you're afraid to try something, should you always try it anyway? Or does God sometimes use fear or uneasiness to protect you from things?

▶What might some of those things be?

▶Are there other times when God wants you to keep trying, even though it's hard? Give some examples from your own life.

18

For God did not give us a spirit of timidity, but a spirit of power, of love and of self-discipline.
(2 Timothy 1:7)

Show me, Lord, if You want to protect me by having me be scared of some things. But help me try again if it's something You want me to learn. Give me the Holy Spirit's power and love and self-discipline. Thank You!

NO ONE WILL KNOW

David had agreed to baby-sit Mick and Tommy Dahlberg, but now he wished he'd stayed at home. The boys gave him trouble right from the start. They wouldn't eat the supper their mom had left for them. They didn't want to change into their pajamas. When David finally got them to bed, they kept asking for water.

At last the boys fell asleep, and David sat down to watch his favorite TV program. As it reached the most exciting point, he heard a key in the lock. The boys' parents were home. He'd miss the end of the show!

"Have a good evening, David?" asked Mr. Dahlberg.

For a moment David hesitated. "Sure," he answered.

"Everything go OK?" asked Mrs. Dahlberg.

"Just fine," David said. "Just fine."

Taking the money Mr. Dahlberg held out, he stuffed it in his jacket pocket. "They can't pay me enough to make *this* evening worth it," he thought.

Not until he reached his own room at home did David unroll the bills. Amazement filled him. "Hmmm, maybe I'm wrong," he muttered. Tucked between the two one-dollar bills was a twenty. "Mr. Dahlberg outdid himself. I'm coming up in the world. Wow! All that money for just one evening's work. Wow!"

Another thought struck him. "With this and what I've saved, would I have enough for that jacket I want? Maybe!"

A moment later his happiness vanished. "Maybe it was a mistake. Maybe Mr. Dahlberg thought he was giving me three ones."

David crawled into bed. "Well, he won't miss the money. They went out to eat. He'll think he lost it somewhere."

David turned out the light, and the room seemed much darker than usual. "I should return the twenty, shouldn't I, God?" But he rejected the idea as quickly as it came.

"Those kids were so awful, I *earned* that money. Maybe God wants to reward me for all my hard work."

For some reason sleep wouldn't come. David rolled over, then back again. The dark seemed to press down on him. "What should I do? Tell Mr. Dahlberg? Or buy that jacket tomorrow?"

TO TALK ABOUT

▶Do you think God was rewarding David for his hard work?

▶Does God use dishonest ways to bless people with money?

▶What will happen if David chooses to keep the twenty dollars and Mr. Dahlberg figures out where it went?

▶How would David feel about himself if he kept the money, even if no one found out?

▶What do you think David did with the twenty dollars?

Once your heart was full of darkness, now it is full of light from the Lord, and your behavior should show it! Because of this light within you, you should do only what is good and right and true. Learn as you go along what pleases the Lord.
(Ephesians 5:8-10, TLB)

Jesus, it's so easy to think that no one will ever know if I just keep things in the dark. But You would know. Help me be honest in the way I live. I want to be pleasing to You.

24

POPCORN
AND...

Allweek Sandy had looked forward to this slumber party. Ever since Amanda invited her she'd thought, "How can I be so lucky? They're the in-group at school. And they asked *me*!"

For a long time she'd wanted to be friends with Amanda and Carol and Katie. Now was her chance!

Standing on the front step of Amanda's house, sleeping bag in one hand and overnight bag in the other, Sandy felt the first twinge of misgiving. She remembered that her friend Erin and three other girls were also having a party that night. She had helped to plan it.

Then came Amanda's invitation, and Sandy decided she would tell Erin that she'd rather be with the other girls. That had been a bad moment.

"Oh," Erin had said. A cloud seemed to enter her clear blue eyes. "Oh. Well, have a good time."

Now Amanda swung the door open wide. "Come on in, Sandy."

Clothes and sleeping bags spread out on the floor, the girls soon gathered in a circle in the family room. "This is great," thought Sandy as she munched chips and popcorn, listening to Carol tell a story. Suddenly everyone laughed. What for? Sandy didn't understand, but pasted a smile on her lips and pretended she did.

Now it was Katie's turn. Her story was long and drawn out. This time Sandy *did* understand. She felt dirty all over. The hotness started inside and crept up into her neck and cheeks. Could they tell how embarrassed she was? It was hard to pretend she was laughing.

"It's your turn, Sandy," said Amanda, giving her a poke. "Let's hear it from Sandy."

"Yaaaaaay!" joined in Carol and Katie. "Ya, rah, rah!"

"I—I—I don't know any," Sandy stuttered.

"Don't know any stories?" Amanda demanded. "Where have you been? In church all your life?"

Sandy swallowed around the lump in her throat. "Yes, that's right. I've been in church." Too embarrassed to meet their gaze, she looked down and began

26

twisting the bottom of her sweatshirt.

"Hey, leave her alone," said Katie. "I go to her church, too."

"You do?" asked Amanda. "But you know more stories than any of us."

Now Katie looked embarrassed. "Well, yes." For a moment she seemed uncomfortable. Then her face brightened as though a joke were coming. "I'm what people call a fence sitter, I guess. One foot in the church and one in the world."

The others laughed, but Sandy felt sick inside. She jumped up, seeking escape in an upstairs bedroom. Delaying as long as she could, she combed her hair at least 100 times. Finally she went back to the family room. Suddenly the conversation stopped.

"Must have been talking about me," thought Sandy. A strange despair made her cold all over. Around her the conversation flowed like a stream swollen by rain in spring. It seemed no one could say anything good about her teachers.

"Well," thought Sandy. "I guess teachers are always fair game. But do they have to go *that* far?" She reached for the popcorn, hoping to cover her discomfort by eating.

The conversation shifted. For some reason everyone kept talking about the girls Sandy usually did things with. First Janie, then Cathy, then Linda.

"They're my friends," she thought. "Until now I

27

never realized how much I like them. But what should I do? Defend them? I'm afraid to."

A moment later the meanness centered on her friend Erin. Sandy could stand it no longer. She jumped up, anger filling every part of her body. "That's not true, that's not true!" she cried out. "She's my best friend. She never did what you said!"

Amanda pulled her back down. "Hey, kid," she said. "What are you getting so excited about?"

Too miserable to answer, Sandy crawled into her sleeping bag. How could something she thought would be so nice be so awful? "This is more than I bargained for. Worst of all, I'm missing out on a party with my *real* friends. Will this terrible night ever end?"

TO TALK ABOUT

▶Do kids in groups other than your own sometimes seem more "in," or more special, than they really are?
▶When God told King Solomon to ask for whatever he wanted, Solomon said, "Give me the wisdom I need to rule your people with justice and to know the difference between good and evil" (1 Kings 3:9, GNB). How can God help us know what people are really like? Perhaps you can remember a time when someone's behavior made you uneasy.
▶Can you think of ways that wisdom might be some-

thing that would offer protection for you?

▶When the party got to be too much for Sandy, she escaped upstairs. What are some other ways we might respond when others tell dirty stories?

▶What do you feel Sandy should tell her friend Erin?

▶What qualities do you value in your best friends?

Whatever you have learned or received or heard from me, or seen in me—put it into practice. And the God of peace will be with you. (Philippians 4:9)

Forgive me, Lord, for wanting something that seems better just because I don't have it. Give me an understanding mind—to know what is good, or not-so-good, or even wrong. Give me friends that help and support me instead of tearing me down. Thank You!

MORE THAN A GAME

Mark glanced around the field in back of his house, then swung into line opposite his three cousins and Uncle Ted. "One more touchdown and we'll have 'em," he thought.

He checked his own line. His older brother, the Hulk, at right end. Sam, another cousin, in front of the pigskin. On the far left, his little sister Celia.

Inwardly he groaned. What could she do? But with Dad gone, they were short one person. Would she remember their secret play?

Hands on knees, Mark crouched. "I wonder what Dad's doing today," he asked himself, as he often did.

With the question came the familiar tightening of his stomach. "I don't think I can stand to eat—not even the big bird," he thought, as his tension grew. "Was it my fault that Dad left? Sometimes he got awfully mad at me."

Every muscle tensed as Mark waited for the ball to be snapped. Yet he couldn't push thoughts of his dad aside. "It's the first Thanksgiving he hasn't played with us."

Sam snapped the ball into Mark's hands. Mark faded back, looking for the Hulk. His brother was racing down the right side, but he was covered.

Mark pivoted. There was Celia on the left, down by the goal line, and completely open. He drew back his arm, and the football made a long spiral through the air.

"Come on, Celia, catch it! Just once," he wanted to shout.

For a long moment she waited, arms in a circle, eyes closed. The ball dropped through her arms like a basketball and hit her stomach. As she hugged the ball, it stayed.

Celia opened her eyes, surprise written across her face.

"Go for it!" shouted Mark. "Over the goal line!"

Turning quickly, Celia took five steps and fell into the end zone.

"Yaaaaaay!" the shout went up. Even the other team hurrahed. Mark and the Hulk slapped Celia on the back. "But Dad isn't here to see it," thought Mark.

"And he won't be cutting the big bird either."

His mother's call interrupted them. "Your dad's on the phone," she said. "You first, Mark. We'll wait to eat."

Fifteen minutes later Mark dropped into his dining room chair and bowed his head. For the first time he had asked his dad, "Was it my fault you and Mom broke up?"

"Of course not, Mark," his dad had said. "It's between your mother and me. I love you as much as I always have, Son."

As Uncle Ted led the prayer, Mark had more to think about than food. "Thank you, God," he prayed, without speaking aloud. "Thank you that my dad still loves me."

Something warm stirred inside him, melting the chunk of ice that had been there for months. Maybe he could eat after all. It was beginning to feel like Thanksgiving.

TO TALK ABOUT

▶Why is it especially hard when someone we love is missing on a holiday?

▶What would have happened to Mark if he hadn't asked, "Dad, was it my fault?"

▶Sometimes misunderstandings come simply because we don't talk enough about what is happening. Can you remember times when you were afraid to speak up and get things sorted out? What happened if you finally told someone how you felt?

▶When you're afraid to talk about things that bother you, how can God help you to speak up?

▶When we have hard times, it helps to thank God for the good things we do have. How did Mark's feelings change as he gave thanks for his dad's love?

"The LORD himself goes before you and will be with you; he will never leave you nor forsake you. Do not be afraid; do not be discouraged."
(Deuteronomy 31:8)

When I don't understand things, Lord, help me to ask questions. When I wonder if I am loved or I feel left behind, put me together with people who will help me. Thank You that You will never leave me. Thank You that You love me always.

34

THE BIG TEST

Spring sunlight warmed the the room as Brian glanced up, searching for a way of escape. Outside, the grass beckoned, and across the schoolyard a lanky boy dropped a basketball in the hoop.

With an effort Brian turned back to his math book. "Do the two problems on page 178," Mrs. Evenson had said. Once again Brian tried to begin.

1. Meyer's Department Store is holding its annual spring sale on many items. Among them are girls' swimsuits. Some that originally sold for $25.00 are being offered at 20% off. Find out how much money the discount is and how much you will have to pay for the swimsuit.

Brian read on, hoping the next question would be easier.

2. Meyer's also has jeans on sale. . . .

Drawing a doodle on the side of his paper, Brian went back to number 1, the tight knot in his head seeming to grow. "Percentages and discounts have always thrown me," he thought. "What am I going to do? Mrs. Evenson wants us to finish before we leave today."

Seemingly in answer to Brian's desperate question, Mrs. Evenson went out into the hall. For a moment Brian waited, wondering how soon she would return. A minute passed. Looking toward the back of the room, Brian cleared his throat. His friend Pam understood. Their gaze met and Pam nodded.

Brian stood up and walked past Pam's desk on the way to the pencil sharpener. Casually he picked up a half-folded piece of paper, sharpened his pencil, and returned to his desk.

Within a few minutes he had copied every answer onto his own paper. Wasting no time, Brian took another trip to the sharpener and dropped Pam's paper where it belonged.

Just as Brian returned to his own desk, Mrs. Evenson came back into the room. "Everyone done?" she asked. "Let's exchange papers and correct them."

From the corner of his eye, Brian watched Jenny as she marked his paper. "100," she wrote in big numbers two inches high. Beneath it, she drew a funny smiling face.

"Poor Jenny," thought Brian. "Doesn't she know I really didn't do it?"

Quickly the boys and girls passed in their math problems. While they cleaned off their desks, preparing to leave, Mrs. Evenson looked at the papers. "Brian," she called. "Could you come up here please?"

His tongue skittering into his boots, Brian stood up. Had Mrs. Evenson found out?

Mrs. Evenson held up Brian's paper. "I want to congratulate you," she said in a voice the whole class could hear. "I know this math is difficult for you, and you've worked so hard that every question is right. I'm proud of you!"

Brian felt his face getting hot, but somehow he smiled. "Thank you, Mrs. Evenson," he said quietly, then returned to his seat.

"Whew!" he thought. "Whew! I made it through that one." But then a thought struck him. "What am I going to do for the test on Friday?"

TO TALK ABOUT

▶What do you think will happen to Brian on Friday?
▶What choice do you feel he should make right now?

How should he act on his choice?
▶Why is it more tempting to cheat if something is really hard to do?
▶What have you found to be better—to take a poor grade, or to cheat? Why?

"Humble yourselves before the Lord, and he will lift you up." (James 4:10)

Lord, I heard once that humbling yourself means confessing your sins. I'm afraid to tell You about the times I've cheated, but I really am sorry about them. Please forgive me. I want to be honest, even when it's hard.

NO LONGER DARK

Mei Ling flicked off the light and took a running leap into bed. Outside, the November wind blew around the corner of her room. Bare branches, stripped of leaves, scratched the side of the house. Back and forth they moved—now blocking the street light, now letting the light shine through.

The wavering light filled the room, sending a shiver through her whole body. Eerie shadows danced on the walls, growing long in corners, melting downward into the stairway outside her door. Feeling all alone and scared, Mei Ling scrunched down under the blankets.

Minutes later Dad came into her room to say

goodnight. He gently pulled the blankets off her head. "Something wrong, Mei Ling? Can I help?"

Afraid to admit her fear of the dark, she shook her head back and forth. But Dad guessed. "Are you afraid of the wind and the dark?"

This time Mei Ling nodded.

"All of us have times when we're afraid," said Dad. "What counts is what we do about it—like choosing to face the reason, for instance."

Going to the door, he flicked on the light switch. The bright light reached into the corners and every shadow melted. For a moment Mei Ling looked around the room, feeling her fear evaporate.

"Now watch," said Dad. He turned off the light and went to the window. "I can pull down the shade if you want." He did so, and the room became dark with no dancing shadows. "But there's something we're missing." With a quick snap, Dad let the shade roll up. "What do you think it is?"

It was a game they'd played before. Dad had showed her how to watch the moods of weather. "The wildness of the November wind," she said.

"What's the wind doing?" prompted Dad.

Mei Ling almost felt like laughing. "Sending the dry, fallen leaves around to find new friends."

Dad hugged her, delighted that she remembered. "Let's read Psalm 121 tonight." Once more he turned on the light.

Mei Ling began reading and her voice grew steadily stronger. "He who watches over you will not slumber; indeed, he who watches over Israel will neither slumber nor sleep."

Moments later Dad turned off the light and left. Mei Ling snuggled down under the blankets. But this time she pulled them only as high as her shoulders. "It's not so bad when I face things," she thought.

Drowsiness settled around her as she repeated to herself, "He who watches over me will not slumber. He will not slumber nor sleep."

TO TALK ABOUT

▶Sometimes we're afraid for a real reason and other times for something we imagine. Which was it for Mei Ling? How did one reason for fear build on top of another?

▶What happened when Mei Ling chose to face her fear and talk about it?

▶ Many people are afraid of the dark. What are some ways to get over that fear?

▶Are there other things that make you afraid? What are they?

▶Often it's necessary to think about a reason for fear long enough to face it. Then, instead of continuing to think about the reason, ask God for help in getting over your fear. If you've memorized Bible verses, you can repeat them when you need power. What are some verses that would be helpful if you're afraid?

"And I will be with you always, to the end of the age." (Matthew 28:20, GNB)

Thank You, Jesus, that when I repeat Bible verses and think about You, my fears go away. Thank You that when I'm afraid, it helps to talk with the right Person—not someone who scares me more. Thank You that You have promised to be with me always.

42

WHICH WAY BACK?

"**J**onathan, you're grounded," said Dad in his I-mean-business voice. "When I ask you to help with dishes, I want you to help. And you don't have to talk back. We're a family. We should be courteous to one another."

Jon stalked out of the room, anger in every cell of his body.

"Don't forget. Stay in the cabin," Dad called after him.

Soon the cabin was quiet. Lying on his bed in the loft, Jon heard his sister and brother and Dad and Mom leave for the boat. From years past he knew what a picnic on the island would be like.

There'd be a heavy basket filled with his favorite

food. The mid-August sun would still be warm. As though he were there, Jon remembered the swimming beach, the sun sparkling on the water, and the feel of sand between his toes.

"If Dad thinks I'm going to stay inside all afternoon, he's got another guess coming," Jon told himself. "I've been wanting to explore the woods around here. I'll do it on my own."

Like a tiny whisper, he seemed to hear Dad's voice. "You're used to living in the city. Don't go into the woods alone. If two of you want to go together, tell us first. Let us know what direction you're taking, and wear your whistles."

"Phooey," Jon answered the inner voice. "I'm not gonna wear a cord with a whistle on it. I'm not a baby. I'll go to the pond we found last summer."

Outside, Jon found the wind had changed, so he returned to the cabin for a sweatshirt. When he couldn't find his own, he snatched up his brother's and pushed it into his backpack. Then he took off through the woods.

He found the pond without difficulty. Clear and still, with only an occasional ripple, the water hugged the shore. Nearby, a stronger current passed into another pond, and a great beaver lodge rose from the surface.

Soon Jon spotted other signs of beavers at work—a large birch with a portion of bark peeled off, and a poplar almost gnawed through. Wood chips surrounded its base. Farther on, Jon saw an even bigger poplar down. Only a sharp, pointed stump remained.

Excitement filled him. "I'd like to have everyone see this. I'll bring 'em back."

A moment later Jon remembered. "I can't. I'll have to pretend I haven't been here." The good feeling about his discovery vanished. "Well, I better get back before they find out I'm gone."

Starting off, he followed the pressed-down line of grass he knew to be a deer path. "Looks like an easier way to the cabin," he thought.

Soon the birch and poplar trees merged into a large pine wood. Jon came to the top of a hill and looked down.

Row after row of tall pine trees stretched as far as he could see. The lower branches had broken off as the upper ones reached for the sun. Beneath them, fallen needles formed a soft, brown carpet.

The wind whispered through the trees as Jon started between them. Here and there a tall pine creaked, as though a squeaky door swung in the wind.

Jon started filling his backpack with cones, then remembered he couldn't take them home. Emptying them out, he started to walk faster, and came to the edge of the pines. Down the hill and off to his right a pond nestled in a hollow.

The sun had disappeared under clouds and the

water looked dark and cold. But somehow the pond seemed. . . .

It was. Around the edge were the trees on which the beavers had gnawed.

The first finger of uneasiness jabbed Jon's ribs. "I've walked in a circle," he told himself. "How do I get home?" He didn't want to admit Dad was right about wearing a whistle.

The hidden sun offered no clue. Trying to push down his fear, Jon started to hurry. "They'll get back and find me gone."

Following the shore, he circled the pond. Stickers clutched at his jeans. Overhanging branches grabbed at his backpack and shirt. Panic filled him.

Starting to run, Jon jumped logs and brushed through tall weeds. Suddenly he stepped in a hole and crashed down.

A sharp flash shot through his ankle. "Ow, ow, ow," he groaned, the whole world seeming to spin. Dizzy with pain, Jon rolled on the ground.

Finally he pushed his elbows into the soft earth and tried to sit up. Every movement was agony.

The rising wind chilled him. He shivered. "It's getting darker and cooler all the time," he thought. "What am I going to *do*? Dad *did* know how big these woods are."

Jon didn't want to admit how scared he felt, but tears of pain and fear pushed against his eyes. For the

first time he regretted what he had done. "Forgive me, God," he prayed. "I'm sorry I didn't do what Dad said."

The scared feeling didn't go away, but at least Jon felt like he could think. Dragging himself on his elbows and good leg, he reached the backpack he had dropped. As he pulled out the sweatshirt, his fingers felt a small, hard object.

Fumbling frantically, Jon felt in the pocket. A moment later he pulled out a long cord. On it, a whistle!

This time Jon didn't think about what Dad would say because he disobeyed. He just felt glad that his family would care about him. "Are they back at the cabin?" he wondered. "Will they hear me?"

With every breath in his body, he blew a long, shrill whistle.

TO TALK ABOUT

▶Do you think Jon's family will find him? Why do you think that?

▶Jon's problem started with not wanting to do dishes. How did one problem build on top of another?

▶Why does sin separate us from God and others?

▶If we tell God we're sorry for our sin, He forgives us. That means because Jon was sorry and asked forgiveness, God forgave him. Yet just because Jon asked forgiveness, does that mean everything suddenly will be all right?

▶Are there times when we have to experience the consequences of what we have done wrong? What are some examples from your own life?

▶How do you think Jon's dad will show his love to Jon?

If we claim to be without sin, we deceive ourselves and the truth is not in us. If we confess our sins, he is faithful and just and will forgive us our sins and purify us from all unrighteousness. (1 John 1:8-9)

Forgive me, Jesus, when I sin against You and other people. I'm sorry for the wrong things I do. Thank You for dying on the cross for my sin. Thank You that when I'm sorry, You forgive me, and help me change.

HOW CAN I LIKE MYSELF?

Paula slid onto a chair, propped her elbows on the table, and leaned forward to close her mouth around a straw. For several moments she looked down, intent on her chocolate milk shake.

Stopping long enough to pick up her spoon, she glanced across at Cindy. There she sat, nice and thin. "Just the perfect weight," thought Paula. "Why do I always look so fat?"

"Oh, oh, big trouble," whispered Cindy. "The guys from school."

Paula bent her head over her chocolate shake, pretending not to see the two boys who came into the ice cream store. Her heart fell to the floor and rolled over as they started in her direction.

Passing too close, the larger boy bumped into her chair. "Sorry, Chubby," he said in a loud voice.

Paula stared at her shake, trying to not let the hurt show in her face.

The boys circled the table. This time the second boy bumped her chair. "Uh-oh, so-o-o s-or-r—*ry!*" he exclaimed, drawling out the words for all they were worth.

Without looking at them, Paula stood up and started for the door. The boys followed. "Running away? Scared of us?"

Paula faced them, her eyes flashing anger. "I'm not scared of you. I can't *stand* you."

She threw down her money and headed out the door. All she wanted was a place to hide—away from the boys, away from staring eyes, away from her own self.

The minute she reached home, Paula went to the kitchen. "I can't stand those boys," she thought.

She looked down at her faded jeans—big across the legs, big across the hips. She pulled out her baggy sweatshirt and sighed. "No matter how big my clothes are, they don't hide how much I weigh. I *want* to be the right weight. I *want* to look good."

One by one she opened the cupboard doors, then slammed them shut. After a search, she found the butterballs her mom had hidden. Sitting down, she began eating first one, then another, then still another.

Finally Paula put the cover back on the cookies. "I can't stand those boys," she thought again. "But most of all, I can't stand myself."

Paula pushed the cookies back into the farthest corner of the cupboard. Even so, she knew she'd find them again.

"Why do I do this?" she asked herself. "Every time something goes wrong, I gobble every dessert I find."

This time her upset feelings took the form of a prayer. "Oh, Lord, how can I start liking myself? Will You help me change?"

TO TALK ABOUT

▶Nearly all of us have something about our bodies that we don't like. We need to accept the way we are or make a change. Is Paula's weight something she needs to accept, or something she needs to change? Why?

▶What people can help her learn better ways to eat?

▶The Holy Spirit can give Paula greater willpower and help her change her eating habits. Yet what choice does Paula need to keep on making, even if she asks the Holy Spirit's help?

▶Why can it also be harmful to a person's health to insist upon being too thin?

▶Is there anything you don't like about yourself?

53

Think carefully about what it is.

▶ Is it something you need to accept? If so, but you keep knocking yourself, what are you telling God about the way He made you? How can you accept yourself in spite of it?

▶ Or do you have something you need to change? How can you start working on it?

▶ If you, like Paula, need new eating habits, what are some ways you can begin making different choices?

I praise you because I am fearfully and wonderfully made; your works are wonderful, I know that full well. (Psalm 139:14)

Thank You, Father, that You created me the way I am. Help me accept the things I need to accept and change the things I should change. Help me avoid things that are bad for me to eat. Give me a desire to eat the right food and the right amount.

PEACE FOR PETE AT CHRISTMAS

Pete took the stairs two at a time, tore into his bedroom, and pulled open the drawers. If he didn't hurry, he'd miss all the fun at the church party.

Yanking open the closet door, he pawed through the shelves, throwing the clothes on the floor. Not there either. In frustration he kicked his wastebasket, sending it flying across the room.

Moments later he entered the kitchen. While his mother cleaned up the dishes, his little sister Janelle shook sparkles on a Christmas decoration and the floor.

"I can't find my red sweater, Mom. And I need to leave."

"Did you wear it and forget to put it away?" she asked.

Pete thought hard. Suddenly he exploded. "*Todd!* I bet Todd took it. Where is he? At the play tryouts? What did he wear?"

"I know," piped up Janelle. "A red sweater and jeans."

"Oh, Mom, how *could* he!" Pete wailed. "He's bigger than I am, and he'll stretch it out. Dumb brother! I hate him."

"*Peter. . . .*"

"I do. I can't stand him."

"I don't blame you for being angry," said Mom. "Todd was wrong, but that isn't a reason to hate him. Why don't you wear something else so you don't miss the party? We'll settle it when you get home."

"Just the same, I hate him," said Pete. "Todd thinks he can take my things whenever he wants."

Pete knew that wasn't true. Yet his anger burned hot all the way to church. Each time he thought about the sweater, it was like adding wood to a bonfire.

His anger cooled as he spotted his best friends around the Christmas tree. But for the first time since he knew the church kids, the games dragged.

"It's all Todd's fault I'm not having fun," Pete thought. "How can I get even with him?"

Near the end of the evening everyone sat down in a circle. The youth leader opened a Bible, read the first verse of the Christmas story, and handed the Bible to the person next to him. Around the circle it came, each one reading a verse.

"Joseph went from the town of Nazareth . . . ."

"There were some shepherds in that part of the country . . . ."

Now it was Pete's turn. In a clear voice he read, "Glory to God in the highest heaven, and peace on earth to those with whom he is pleased!" (Luke 2:14, GNB).

Pete started thinking. "Peace on earth. . . ." He tried to brush it aside, but couldn't. "Peace on earth?"

Suddenly he felt ashamed. "Sure, Todd did something wrong," he thought. "But what about me? I've wasted the whole evening being mad at my brother."

"What should I do?" he wondered. "Hold it over his head for the next six months? Or tell Todd I forgive him?"

TO TALK ABOUT

▶ Do you think Pete will forgive Todd, or will he remind Todd about the sweater every chance he gets?

▶ When Pete gets home, Mom can be referee. But why would it be better if Pete and Todd talk with each other and settle the problem themselves?

▶ Some people say, "Forgive and forget," but it's not

always easy. Why is it so hard sometimes?

▶ If you forgive others in spite of how they hurt you, how can God begin to work in your life?

▶ Can you think of any examples from your past?

▶ If a person keeps on taking advantage of you by taking your things without permission, what can you do?

"If you forgive others the wrongs they have done to you, your Father in heaven will also forgive you."
(Matthew 6:14, GNB)

In Your name, Jesus, I forgive the people who have hurt me. Thank You that when I forgive others, You forgive me for the wrong things I have done. Help me to talk to the people who make me mad. Help us to forgive each other and solve our problems.

JUST A MINUTE, MOM

Mr. Wallin stopped Greg on the way to his desk. "I want to talk with you."

Greg's breath caught. "Here it comes," he thought. "Just what I've been dreading."

Mr. Wallin opened his grade book. "Whenever I assign something to be done outside of class, you hand it in late. Your work is good. It's just as hard to do it later on, and I have to give you a lower grade. Why don't you get it in on time?"

Greg looked down. How could he tell Mr. Wallin that he hated homework so much that he always put it off?

After a long moment of silence, Mr. Wallin spoke again.

"You're forming a habit that will hurt you the rest of your life. I'll have to talk to your mother."

Greg's head jerked up. "Oh, don't do that."

"I don't have any choice. You need to learn responsibility."

That afternoon Greg dreaded going home. He didn't want to add something more to the load his mom was carrying. Yet he didn't know how to change things either. What would Mom say?

He was watching TV near the kitchen when his mother came home with groceries. Greg barely glanced up. Bringing in the third bag she asked, "Can you help me put these away, Greg?"

"Just a minute, Mom," he answered, his gaze never leaving the TV screen.

The heavy thud of the bag on the counter caught Greg's attention, and he looked up. For some reason his mother's shoulders sagged more than usual. As she moved between the counter and the refrigerator, she looked tired.

Uneasiness tightened Greg's throat. A twinge of shame touched him. For the first time he noticed the lines around his mother's eyes. "You okay, Mom?" he asked.

His mother slumped into a chair. "No, I'm not. They keep giving me longer and harder reports at work. At least I finished the worst one so I don't have to figure it out tomorrow. When I get something I don't like to do, I tell myself, 'Do it first. Get it behind you.' And I did."

Her look of discouragement deepened. "Mr. Wallin called me at work. I'm disappointed with you, Greg. You're having the same problem both here and at school. . . ."

She broke off and started again. "I wish you'd change this pattern of putting things off."

"Ahhhh, Mom," Greg answered. "I just don't feel like doing homework after I've been in school all day. And I don't feel like doing things around here."

"Just the same, get started by putting away the groceries while I make supper. I'm tired."

After supper Greg dropped down in front of the TV again. He knew he should clean up the kitchen, but he didn't feel like it. Nor did he feel like starting his homework.

His mother interrupted Greg's concentration. "Do the dishes, won't you? Don't you have homework?"

Greg barely glanced up. A sound of defeat entered his mother's voice. "Greg, I'm going to bed early. And I'm not going to nag anymore. From now on it's up to you."

The TV program was better than usual, but a tape of Mr. Wallin's voice kept replaying, "You're forming a habit that will hurt you. Hurt you. Hurt you." Each time the thought returned, Greg pushed it down.

The program ended, and he switched channels.

Three hours later Greg fell asleep in front of the TV.

Early morning light wakened him. Cold and stiff from lying on the sofa without a blanket, Greg remembered his homework and the dirty dishes. "Oh, no!" he thought. "I'll get it again." A sudden, panicky feeling clutched his stomach. "Why do I always do this? The dishes will be twice as hard to wash. Mr. Wallin will be mad again."

Greg sat up, his feeling of dread deepening. "I hate myself for not getting things done. But how do I change?"

Like a song going around in his head, he remembered his mother's words: "Do it first. Get it behind you." Greg glanced at the clock. An hour before he needed to dress for school.

"Should I do my homework?" he asked himself. "Should I even clean up the kitchen? Or should I crawl into bed?"

TO TALK ABOUT

▶What choice do you think Greg made?

▶What does it mean to take responsibility for doing something?

▶How can TV or a video game offer an excuse to put things off?

▶Is it easier to wait to do something, or to do it right away? Why?

▶What are some ways God uses little tests to train you to be a responsible, trustworthy person?

"For I know the plans I have for you," declares the LORD, "plans to prosper you and not to harm you, plans to give you hope and a future."
(Jeremiah 29:11)

Help me, Lord, when I'm tempted to put things off. I want to be a person others can trust. Help me form good habits so You can use me in those plans You have for me.

63

I DARE YOU!

Kelly yawned and looked up at the hands of the clock. With a new boy in school, it had been an exciting day. Yet now time seemed to have stopped.

Finally the hands moved on, minute by minute. Kelly couldn't wait to be in the sun, free as a breeze.

Jill, the most popular girl in the room, had chosen *her*, Kelly. Amy, the second most popular girl, was coming along. Sure, it was longer to walk home the way they chose, but it was worth it.

At last the moment came. Surrounded by a hundred other kids, they pushed their way out the school door and started down the street. Soon they left the others behind.

Jill giggled. "Didn't you like the new boy who started today? I just love Rob's brown eyes. And his muscles—*wow!*"

She tossed her head, and her blond hair bounced around her shoulders. "Did you see the way he watches me? I think he likes me."

To Kelly, the bright sunshine suddenly seemed covered by clouds. Twice Rob had spoken to her that morning. When they traded test papers, he smiled at the funny mark she used for corrections. He liked the cartoon she drew at the bottom. She had wondered, "Could he really like me?" But now Jill had said. . . .

Kelly ached inside. "How can I make Rob like me?" she thought. "What can I do to be as popular as Jill?"

Just then Jill opened her backpack. "Look! I've got half a pack of cigarettes my mom left out. Let's cut down this street, and no one will see us."

Kelly stopped in her tracks. "No, I don't think so."

"Oh, come on," said Jill. "I've smoked before, and it's really neat."

"I've tried it too," said Amy. "It won't hurt you any."

"Then why do they put that warning on cigarettes?" asked Kelly.

"That's just for people who aren't strong," answered Jill. "Nothing will happen to *you.*"

"Sorry," said Kelly. "It's too hard to stop smoking. I don't want to start."

"I dare you," answered Amy. "I double-dare you!"

"Sissy!" said Jill. "You'll never be popular that way."

Kelly cringed. Her mixed-up feelings seemed like the tumbling of a waterfall. She wanted to cry out, "I *like* you. I don't want you to die of lung cancer the way my uncle did." But somehow the words stuck in her throat.

She wondered if Jill and Amy could see how hot her face felt. "Is this what it means to be popular?" she asked herself. "If I say no, does it mean I can't be their friend anymore?"

TO TALK ABOUT

▶What do you think Kelly will do?

▶If she says no, what will Jill and Amy do?

▶Is it important to be popular with everyone? Why do you think so?

▶Do you think God ever allows us to be *un*popular? What are some reasons why?

▶The Bible shows us how God wants us to live. If you are tempted to do something wrong, what Bible verses or stories can help you make the right choice?

"Don't be afraid! Stand your ground, and you will see what the LORD will do to save you today."
(Exodus 14:13, GNB)

When I'm tempted to do wrong things, take away my fear, Lord. Help me to say no, and to stand my ground. Help me show the kids who tempt me that I still like them, even though I don't go along with what they do. Thank You that I don't have to choose wrong things in order to be popular.

68

THE NEW BABY

When Eric went to the hospital to see his new baby brother, it was fun. "Here he is!" said Dad, putting the blanket-wrapped bundle in Eric's arms. "Jeremy Daniel!"

"He looks just like you did," said Mom.

Eric's friend Ozzie had told him all about new babies. But Eric couldn't see much of this one—only the blanket, a shock of hair, and a tiny face. The sleeping baby didn't seem like a brother at all. "He's so *little!*" said Eric.

"Yep, he is," answered Dad. "But he'll grow fast. Before you know it, you can toss a ball to him."

Eric doubted it, but just then the baby yawned and opened his eyes. Mom pulled the blanket aside so

Eric could see Jeremy's arms and legs. As he waved a little fist, he looked like he was saying hi.

Eric laughed at the weird expression on Jeremy's face. "Did I really look like that? His skin is so red and wrinkly."

But when Mom brought Jeremy home from the hospital, Eric discovered it wasn't quite so much fun. Often the baby cried at night. Sometimes he woke Eric up. And then there was the company! Everyone brought a present and gathered around the baby.

"All that red hair!" said one lady. "What a good-looking boy!"

"He's good-looking?" Eric asked himself. He didn't dare to say what he really thought.

But in the week that followed, everyone agreed with the lady. Not only was Jeremy good-looking. Not only did he have lots of red hair. He was also the perfect weight, and the perfect size, and the perfect baby! Everyone talked only about Jeremy.

Then one day Aunt Meg and several of Mom's friends came over. When Mom brought out Jeremy, they passed him from one person to another. By that time Eric had had enough.

"Ooooooh! Ahhhhh!" he thought. That wasn't what they said, but they might just as well have. He felt left out and decided to hunt up his friend Ozzie.

As Eric headed for the door one of the ladies asked, "Isn't Jeremy a nice brother?" But she went on talking before Eric could give her an answer.

Then Aunt Meg spotted him. "Hey, Eric, what've you been doing lately?"

Usually Eric liked Aunt Meg, but today he didn't feel like talking to anyone. When he managed to slip outside, he took his bike from the garage and went for a long ride. Along the way he found Ozzie.

He didn't want to tell Ozzie how he felt, but Eric was so quiet that Ozzie guessed.

"Aw, they'll be over it soon," said Ozzie. "That's the way moms act about a new baby. I should know."

Ozzie knew all right. With three kid sisters he was an expert on babies.

"And you don't need to feel jealous," said Ozzie. "I used to. But look at all the stuff I can do that my sisters can't. They just have to be around Mom all the time."

Eric was starting to feel better. But still he didn't like the way his life had changed.

When he finally returned home, Mom asked, "Where've you been? Aunt Meg wanted to talk with you more, but we couldn't find you."

Mom looked tired as she stood by the stove, jiggling the baby in one arm. With her other hand she stirred the stew for supper. Jeremy yowled.

Eric remembered the days when Mom always seemed bouncy. She hadn't looked bouncy for a long time. Right now she looked like she wanted to cry along with Jeremy.

"Mom," he said, then stopped.

"What, Eric?"

Eric was afraid to ask, but he needed to know. "Is it sometimes hard for you to have Jeremy?"

Mom looked like she was thinking. "Yes, I guess I'd have to say that sometimes it is."

"Was it ever hard for you to have me?"

Again Mom looked thoughtful. "Yes, sometimes it was. But I loved you so much it was worth it." She grinned. "Don't you agree? You turned out pretty well!" Leaving the stove, she gave Eric a hug with her free arm.

In that moment something broke loose inside Eric. Something that had been hurting ever since the baby came home. He felt strange—almost free again—as if he'd been let out of school for vacation.

Since that day in the hospital he hadn't held Jeremy. He hadn't wanted to. Now Eric felt surprised by his own words. "Do you want me to hold him?"

Mom's smile erased the tired lines around her eyes. As soon as Eric sat down, she put the baby on his lap.

In that instant Jeremy looked up and stopped crying. He seemed to be checking Eric out.

At first Eric felt afraid to move. He just held the baby, glad that Jeremy seemed to like him. Then, after a few minutes, Eric decided to try something. With one finger he rubbed the palm of Jeremy's hand, the way he'd seen Mom do. Jeremy's little fingers closed around Eric's bigger one. Then the baby's lips parted and curved up at the corners.

"Hey, he smiled!" exclaimed Eric.

"Sure enough! That's his first smile," said Mom. "And he gave it to you!"

Eric leaned back in the chair and made himself comfortable. "Maybe it won't be so bad having a brother after all," he thought.

TO TALK ABOUT

▶At first Eric felt jealous of his little brother. What does it mean to feel jealous? How did feeling jealous affect the way Eric acted toward Jeremy?

▶What choice did Eric make? How did that choice bring a change in what was happening?

▶Eric didn't tell his mom or dad how he felt about the new baby. One way to start would be to say, "I feel" and finish the sentence. He could use a word that describes feelings, such as "glad" or "sad" or "mad" or whatever he felt. What do you think Eric could say to his mom?

▶Why is it important for Eric's mom to know his feelings?

▶When you have bad feelings, it doesn't mean you're a bad person. But it's important not to ignore your feelings. When you talk to the right person, it helps you sort things out. What people in your life can you talk to? Have they ever helped you sort things out? How?

▶When we talk about how we feel, we also find new ways to solve a problem. Is there a problem in your life you'd like to talk about? What is it?

My God will meet all your needs according to his glorious riches in Christ Jesus. (Philippians 4:19)

Jesus, sometimes I'm all mixed up. When I feel that way, help me to talk about my feelings with the right person. Thank You that when I do, I get things sorted out. Thanks that I feel much better.

MANDY COMES TO BAT

"Let's go to the baseball diamond at the park," said Mandy.

"Let's not, and say we did," answered Brad, tossing a softball in the air.

Mandy tried again. "My dad said we're not supposed to play in the street."

"Ah, come on, Mandy, the park is too far away," Brad told her.

Mandy still had her doubts. After all, she was the one with the most to lose. She lived here, while the others came from blocks farther away.

"Hey, Mandy, do you wanna play or don't ya?" called another boy.

"Well," Mandy started to give in. "Put first base a

few more feet that way." She pointed along the curb. "Mrs. O'Rourke is crabby. She doesn't want us on her grass."

They moved first base onto another neighbor's lawn, and started playing. Soon Mandy came up to bat.

Brad was pitching, and Mandy knew he'd give her his fastest ball. Taking a firm grip on the bat, she waited. Sure enough, there it came—a little low, but right over the plate.

Mandy swung and connected. A fly popped off to the right. Then C-R-A-A-A-S-S-H! The sound of broken glass shattered the air.

Mandy looked around and felt sick. Sure enough, it was Mrs. O'Rourke's window.

One moment everyone looked toward the porch. The next instant every kid scattered in a different direction.

Every kid, that is, except Mandy. She felt frozen to the spot. Then, as she recovered, she headed for the bushes across the street. Just in time she knelt down, hiding behind the leaves and peering through.

Mrs. O'Rourke opened her front door. Cane in hand, she came out slowly. She still looked slender and tall with her white hair piled on top of her head. But Mandy knew it was difficult for her to walk. Today she leaned on her cane more than usual.

Mrs. O'Rourke looked at the shattered glass, then

turned to the empty street. Her face crumpled.

The sick feeling in Mandy's stomach grew. Waiting behind the bushes, she knew she could get away. "She might guess, but she can't prove I did it," thought Mandy. "After all, a lot of kids were here."

Mrs. O'Rourke moved and her cane seemed to slip on the glass. Still Mandy waited, afraid Mrs. O'Rourke would be mad.

"Why should I take the blame?" Mandy asked herself. "All the kids were in on it."

As she watched, Mrs. O'Rourke stretched out her cane, and her feet followed. Slowly she went back into the house.

Mandy backed away from the bushes that hid her. On her hands and knees she crept to the corner of the nearby house. But instead of edging away to safety, she waited a minute.

Everything within Mandy wanted to run. At the same time, something held her there. Most of all, she felt ashamed.

Finally, feeling as if her feet were not her own, Mandy stood up and walked into the open. Crossing the street, she dragged her feet up Mrs. O'Rourke's steps and rang the bell.

"I'm crazy," she thought as she waited. "What will I say?"

Mrs. O'Rourke opened the screen door, and Mandy waited for the angry words she thought she'd hear.

Instead, Mrs. O'Rourke spoke quietly.

"Hello, Mandy."

Mandy looked down at the weather-beaten boards of the porch. The boards were gray with time, and Mandy wondered if other kids had ever stood where she did. Then she drew a deep breath and looked up, facing Mrs. O'Rourke's faded blue eyes.

"I'm sorry," she said. She wanted to tell Mrs. O'Rourke it was the other kids' fault. She wanted to put the blame on them. But only four words stumbled out. "I broke your window."

"I know," said Mrs. O'Rourke to Mandy's surprise. "I saw you out another window, just before the ball hit. I was going to call your dad at his office."

Mandy's gaze fell to the old porch once more. "What if she'd been standing at the window I broke?" she thought, full of misery.

"I'm sorry," said Mandy again.

"I forgive you," said Mrs. O'Rourke quietly. "I respect you for coming. I know that was hard for you."

Suddenly Mandy's gaze found the older woman's eyes. Something Mandy saw there drew her to Mrs. O'Rourke. "Why have I always thought she's crabby?" she wondered.

Aloud she said, "What can I do to pay for the window?"

Mrs. O'Rourke pushed the screen door farther open. "Why don't you come in? We'll talk about it."

Mandy drew a deep breath. For some strange reason she almost felt like she had a new friend.

TO TALK ABOUT

▶ The story tells some of the feelings Mandy had about the broken window. How do you feel when you do something wrong and don't want to own up to it?

▶ Mandy made more than one choice. Instead of running away, she went to Mrs. O'Rourke. When she apologized, she also looked Mrs. O'Rourke in the eye. Why would that be important to the older woman?

▶ Mandy was very direct. She said, "I'm sorry," instead of putting the blame on the other kids. Why is it important that Mandy took that responsibility? What does it mean to take responsibility for something?

▶ Mrs. O'Rourke did some special things for Mandy. What were they?

▶ If Mrs. O'Rourke had acted mean instead, what do you think Mandy would have said or done? If someone like Mandy was treated in a mean way, what would you say to encourage that person?

▶ If someone apologizes to you, why is it important to tell that person, "I forgive you"?

▶ What do you suppose Mandy and Mrs. O'Rourke decided about the broken window? What would you do if you were Mandy?

The LORD . . . does not refuse any good thing to those who do what is right (Psalm 84:11, GNB)

Jesus, when I've done something wrong, help me to do the right thing. Help me to own up to what I did and say I'm sorry. Thank You that whenever I ask forgiveness, You do forgive me.

ADAM AND THE BULLY

Adam glanced over his shoulder. "Uh-oh," he thought.

Not far behind in the crowded hallway, Eddie was moving up, all 150 pounds of him. Even from this distance, Adam could hear him laughing with his buddy Dale.

Adam turned toward his locker, pretending he didn't see. Clutching his books under one arm, he started twirling the combination lock. "I hate that big bully," he thought.

It wasn't hard to remember how Eddie had belted him once. And Adam was still sore where he'd been kicked in the leg. "Maybe Eddie won't notice me this time," he thought.

83

The next moment Adam felt a jolt from behind. His books flew out from beneath his arm. Papers scattered in every direction.

Adam whirled to face Eddie. "You big bully!" he shouted. "Who do you think you are?"

Eddie moved forward, his fists clenched. But Adam held his ground.

Just then Dale stepped between them. "Hey, Eddie, what did you do that for?"

"For the fun of it," answered the bigger boy. "Just to watch the splatter. Pretty good, huh?"

"Pretty dumb," said Dale. "Some fun. Come on. Forget it."

They moved off down the hall, and Adam felt relieved. Yet he also felt worthless, like a clod of dirt beneath Eddie's feet.

As Adam picked up his books and papers, the anger within him grew. That anger still burned at suppertime when he told Mom and Dad what happened.

"Eddie?" asked his mom. "Does he have any friends?"

"Dale," answered Adam. "But even Dale didn't like him today."

"Eddie sounds like a very unhappy person," said Dad.

"Wellll—I guess I never thought about it," said Adam. "I just know I can't stand him."

"If not even his friend likes the way he acts, what does he do for fun?" asked Dad.

"I don't know," said Adam. "And I don't care."

Just then a light crossed Mom's face. "Uh oh," thought Adam. "One of her bright ideas, I suppose."

"Why don't you invite Eddie to your birthday party?" she asked.

"Aw, Mom, you gotta be kidding! Do you know what he'd do? He'd wreck the whole thing."

"I don't think so," said Dad quietly. "Your mother might have something there."

"I can't believe what you're saying!" said Adam. "I should invite the meanest kid I know?"

"Well, maybe so," said Dad.

"But I'm supposed to have *fun* at my birthday party!" exclaimed Adam.

"It might turn out to be just that," replied Dad.

"Oh, *Dad!*"

"Why don't you think about it?" he asked.

"I'll think, all right. I can't think of anything that would be worse." Adam pushed back his chair to leave the table.

"Just a minute, Son," said Dad. "Let's have devotions before you leave." He slid a box of Bible verses forward. "We'll each pick a verse tonight."

Adam wanted to escape, but slowly pulled out a card. "Oh, no," he thought, as he read what it said. He hoped Mom and Dad would forget his turn, but they didn't. He had no choice but to read aloud. "If your enemy is hungry, feed him; if he is thirsty, give him something to drink. . . . Do not be overcome by evil, but overcome evil with good" (Romans 12:20-21).

Mom and Dad laughed. Adam didn't. "I said I'd think about it," he protested, the anger rising in his voice. "What am I supposed to do?"

Adam pushed the whole thing to the back of his mind until the next day. When he saw Eddie in the hall, he remembered what Mom and Dad had suggested. Yet every feeling within Adam shouted no.

Once again he tried to avoid Eddie, but couldn't. As Eddie edged up, Adam stepped back. But in the next instant a thought came to him. "Why don't I invite Eddie and be really mean to him? I could do it so Mom and Dad wouldn't know. They'd get off my back, and I'd still win."

For a moment he considered the idea. "What can I do to get even?"

A secret glee welled up inside him, and Adam straightened to his full height. He still came only to Eddie's shoulder, but his words sounded strong and sure. "Eddie, do you want to come to my birthday party on Saturday? We're gonna play broomball, and Mom's fixing lots of food."

Eddie's face had a strange look. "You want me to come?" he asked.

"Sure," said Adam, not really meaning it. But

before Saturday he should be able to think of the biggest chunk of meanness ever invented. "Two o'clock, okay? And bring a broom. We'll play on the rink across the street from my house."

For the first time, Adam dreaded his birthday party. One part of him looked forward to getting even with Eddie. The other part hated himself for what he was going to do.

Adam and his friends were already on the ice when Eddie showed up. He stood at the edge of the rink, his stubby, sawed-off broom in his hand. He looked as though he didn't know what to do.

"I'll pretend I don't see him," thought Adam. "I'll treat him like he's crashing the party. Then I'll let him play, and we'll all gang up on him."

For the next ten minutes Adam stuck to his plan, making sure he didn't glance in Eddie's direction. Yet in a break between plays he couldn't help but see the lost look on Eddie's face.

"Is that how I look when Eddie is mean to me?" Adam asked himself. For a moment he felt a sliver of sympathy for Eddie, but he pushed it aside. "I hope he's wondering if this is all a trick."

Two plays later Adam decided it was time for Plan B. "Come here, Eddie," he called. "You can be on my team."

The players took their positions. Adam moved out, his broom extended like a hockey stick. The ball shot toward him. His broom connected, and the ball slid into the net.

Time after time Adam took control of the ball. It seemed he could do no wrong. The score for his team mounted.

But Eddie was having trouble. Somehow his arms and legs moved in opposite directions. More than once he landed flat on the ice and everyone hooted. Often he looked embarrassed. As Eddie picked himself up, he glanced at Adam, as though he wondered what Adam thought.

"He's clumsy," Adam decided. "Is it possible Eddie's never played before? I'm surprised he keeps trying."

A small cut above Eddie's eye was bleeding. A secret smugness filled Adam. "What will happen when we gang up on him?" he wondered. "Eddie's so awkward he won't have a chance."

Once more the ball shot out. Eddie went after it, stretching out his legs. As he took a swing, he fell hard and slid into the net. The net collapsed around him.

The other boys roared with laughter, but the discomfort of shame broke through Adam's desire for revenge. One part of himself said, "I want to get even." The other part asked, "Should I help him? What will the other kids think?"

Finally he drew a deep breath. "I'll probably hate myself for this." Moving forward, he offered his hand

and helped Eddie up. Eddie looked surprised.

Inside, Adam felt just as surprised about what he had done. Then he felt good.

TO TALK ABOUT

▶ Most people know someone who is mean to them at least now and then. When someone treats you that way, how does it make you feel?

▶ When you've tried to be kind, and it turns out well, how do you feel?

▶ Adam found one way to "feed" his enemy and "give him something to drink." How did Adam "overcome evil with good"?

▶ How do you think Eddie acted during the rest of the party? How do you suppose Adam and Eddie acted toward each other the next time they met?

▶ Is there a kid in your life who acts mean the way Eddie did with Adam? What are some ways you can show kindness to that bully?

▶ If that person continues to take advantage of you, what should you do?

Do not be overcome by evil, but overcome evil with good. (Romans 12:21)

Jesus, when kids are mean, I just want to crawl in a hole. I want to hate them. I have a hard time believing I would be able to do what Adam did. But help me, Jesus. Show me how to act toward those who are mean to me.

NEVER GOOD ENOUGH

"I'm afraid to see my report card," thought Vicki. "I've never worked so hard in my life. If my grades aren't better, I'll feel like giving up."

A moment later the teacher stopped by Vicki's desk, and her warm smile offered hope. As she saw her grades, Vicki wanted to shout. She could barely keep the good news inside.

Walking home, Vicki hugged her best friend. "Wow! Do you know what? I got three Bs and one A. I've never done so well. I can't believe it!"

Rachel hugged her back. "You really studied, Vicki. You earned those grades. I'm proud of you!"

A warm satisfaction filled Vicki until she felt like a

pop can ready to fizz over. The feeling stayed with her as she reached the house and found her mom home early from work. Walking into the kitchen, Vicki discovered things were not going well for Mom.

"Hi, Vicki," she said. "Put away your things, okay? Sandbergs will be here in two hours."

"Sure, Mom, but I want to show you my grades. . . ."

"Not right now. I have to get this meat in the oven, and the veggies ready, and the table set. . . ."

"But, Mom, it just takes a minute. I want you to see. I got three Bs and one A."

"That's nice, Vicki. Now go clean the bathroom for me. When you're done with that, vacuum the hall."

Vicki walked slowly to her bedroom. Some of the fizz had gone out of her day. All that work, and Mom didn't even hear what she said. Well, maybe Dad would be interested.

As Vicki finished vacuuming, Dad came in. "Hi, Pumpkin," he said with a quick hug.

As he walked down the hall, Vicki stopped him. "I got my grades today, Dad. I think you'll like them. I worked as hard as I could, just like you said."

Dad waited while Vicki got her report card. "See? Isn't that great?"

"Hmmm," said Dad as Vicki anxiously watched his face.

"I just want to know he cares," she thought. "That's all I need. If only he would tell me that he likes what I did, all the work will be worth it."

"Hmmmm," said Dad again. Then he looked up. "I bet if you'd really tried you could have gotten all As."

The can of pop inside Vicki fizzed out. Taking the report card, she walked quietly to her bedroom, blinking away the tears. Dad didn't seem to notice.

Once she was alone the torrent came. "Oh, God!" Vicki cried out. "I tried so hard. I studied, and studied, and it wasn't enough. I wanted them to be proud of me. Whatever I do, it's never good enough."

Vicki's shoulders shook as she cried into her pillow so Mom and Dad wouldn't hear. Like a bike wheel spinning very fast, the words went round and round in her head. "Not good enough. Not good enough. Not good enough."

Finally Vicki blew her nose. "Should I stop trying? Should I give up? What's the use?"

Then a new thought came to Vicki. "God, You know I really tried, don't You? What do *You* think about my grades? Are they good enough for You?"

TO TALK ABOUT

▶ If you could talk to Vicki about her three Bs and one A, what would you say?

▶ Vicki knows she has done her best. What is more important—how she feels about her grades or how someone else reacts? Why do you think so?

▶Why do all of us especially want to be noticed and approved of by our parents or others close to us?

▶When those people don't seem to care about us, what can bring us comfort?

▶What do you suppose God thinks about the work Vicki did? How can she choose to concentrate on that?

"The LORD your God is with you, he is mighty to save. He will take great delight in you, he will quiet you with his love, he will rejoice over you with singing."
(Zephaniah 3:17)

Jesus, it means so much to me when the people I love tell me I'm doing great. Yet even if they don't encourage me, help me do my best. Thank You that You always care about me and about what I do. Thank You that You'll never leave me or forget me.

94

A LOOK IN THE MIRROR

Shelly hated using the mirror in the school bathroom. The light gave her skin a funny color. Every spot and blemish showed. And today she felt even more critical of her appearance than usual.

Taking out her brush, she tried once more to bring her hair over the zits on her forehead. "No matter what I do, I can't hide them," she thought.

Next she inspected her eyes. "I wish I had big brown ones like Sarah Leamington. How can I ever be popular the way I look?"

Gazing intently at herself, Shelly barely noticed the girl who had come in. Then a strange movement in the mirror caught Shelly's attention.

"What's she doing?" Shelly wondered. "Straightening her *hair*? Did she slide it around on her head?"

Without moving, Shelly watched the girl's reflection. Strange. The girl held onto her hair as she brushed it!

Suddenly Shelly realized the girl in the mirror was watching her. Red crept into Shelly's face. She'd been caught staring. "Oh, wow!" she thought. "There I go again—forgetting how someone else might feel."

Picking up her books, Shelly turned to go, but something clicked in her mind. The girl with cancer. She had just started two of Shelly's classes. Everyone had been talking about her and the chemotherapy [kee-mo-ther-a-pee] she was taking. Some even said she'd lost her hair and wore a wig. The rumor must be true.

Shelly turned back just in time to see a tear rolling down the girl's cheek. Other tears followed. The silent weeping made Shelly feel terrible. "Should I say something?" she wondered. "Or pretend I don't notice?"

For a moment she stood there, trying to decide. The girl acted as if she didn't see her. At last Shelly spoke. "I'm Shelly Erickson. What's your name?"

The girl's lips quivered. "Jeanine," she said. "Jeanine O'Brien." Bending over, she turned on a faucet and splashed cold water on her face. "I'll be all right," she mumbled.

Still Shelly hesitated before she spoke. "I don't

know what's wrong, but can I help?"

For the first time, Jeanine turned to face her. "Help? I wish you could." If the words hadn't sounded so hopeless, Shelly would have thought she was bitter. Instead, Jeanine seemed ready to give up.

"What's wrong?" Shelly asked.

Jeanine turned back to the sink. The tears started again. "I've never been so embarrassed. Both yesterday and today. . . ." She leaned over, and braced herself against the sink, as though unable to stand up anymore.

Shelly waited, feeling embarrassed herself. She didn't like being uncomfortable.

Jeanine drew a long, ragged breath. "The boys found out . . ." she struggled for self-control, and still Shelly waited.

"The boys found out I'm wearing a wig. When I walk through the hall, they come up behind me and pull it off and. . . ."

"Oh, no!" thought Shelly. "And I didn't like my hair and the color of my eyes."

Jeanine's shoulders shook with sobs, but no sound escaped. Shelly stood there, wondering what to do.

Finally Jeanine spoke. "I can't walk down that hall again. Taking chemo is bad enough. But I can't handle how the boys laugh when they see my bald head."

"Oh, God," Shelly prayed. "Maybe Mom is right

when she tells me to stop spending so much time at the mirror! Forgive me, God."

Once again Jeanine turned on the faucet and splashed her face.

Shelly wanted to run. Instead, she prayed silently. "Jesus, I don't know what to do. You're going to have to show me. Help!"

Jeanine straightened up, drew a deep breath, and looked in the mirror. Again she took out her wire brush. Holding the wig with one hand, she used the other to tease a strand down over her forehead.

She tried to smile, but her lips trembled. "Well, how do I look?"

"Great!" Shelly said. But inside she hurt, thinking how it must feel to be bald. "Let's figure out what we can do."

"I've tried," said Jeanine. "I don't want to stay home all day. I need something to do. I want to be here with kids, but...."

Shelly had an idea. "You said the boys come up behind you? Okay, then *I'm* going to walk behind you."

"You mean ...?" For the first time Shelly saw hope in Jeanine's eyes.

When Shelly spoke, her voice sounded more confident than she felt. "Yep. I'll walk behind you whenever you go through the hall. I'll make sure none of the boys get near you."

Jeanine looked as if she wanted to believe her, but wasn't sure she could.

Shelly kept on. "You're in two of my classes, so I'll walk with you before and after. I'll talk to the other girls, and we'll work out a system for your other classes."

Jeanine smiled, and it was like the sun coming out after a storm.

Shelly laughed. "We'll fool 'em," she said.

Jeanine straightened her shoulders, as if for battle. With Shelly behind her, she walked into the hall.

TO TALK ABOUT

▶ How do you think Shelly will feel about herself the next time she looks in the mirror? In what ways can you be thankful about your own appearance?

▶ There's a difference between showing pity and giving understanding. Showing pity means we act as if we're sorry for someone, but wouldn't want to be like them. We offer syrupy words, but no real help. What might have happened to Jeanine if Shelly had treated her that way?

▶ Giving understanding means that we let someone know we feel sorry about what's happening to them, but we also offer support. In what way did Shelly give understanding to Jeanine?

▶ Understanding helps a person go on, even though

it's hard. Pity takes away whatever hope or self-confidence a hurting person has left. Why was it important to Jeanine that she keep going to school?

▶Have there been times when you've made fun of someone? If you could, how would you change that now?

▶While Jesus lived on earth, He showed that He cared about what happened to people. How did He also help them in practical ways? Look for clues in Mark 6:30-44 and John 11:32-44.

"You answered me when I called to you; with your strength you strengthened me." (Psalm 138:3, GNB)

Jesus, it's so easy to be selfish and think only about myself. I choose to think about the hurts and needs of people around me. Help me to love them with Your love and find practical ways to help.

100

LATE FOR SUPPER

"Bye, Steve. See you tomorrow," called Blake. The door closed behind him. A moment later it popped open again.

"Hey, Blake, wait a minute. I forgot to show you my new rocket."

Blake turned and leapfrogged back up the steps. He shared Steve's enthusiasm for rocket-building. Yet he felt uneasy, and kept glancing at his watch.

Finally he pulled away. "I really have to go. I promised Mom I'd be home at 4:30, and it's already 5."

This time Blake half-walked, half-ran down the sidewalk. Early January twilight shut him into a gray-blue world. Ahead of him the street light turned on. Soon it would be dark.

"I'll head down Main Street," he thought. "It's a block longer, but there will be more lights and people."

Passing the gas station and post office, he started to jog. Just then he heard a shout. "Hey, wait for me!"

A moment later Dan caught up to him. "Come here, Blake. I want you to see something."

Blake shook his head. "I'm already late. I promised. . . ."

"It'll just take a minute. I want you to see the new ten-speeds O'Connell's got in. Come on. You'll like them."

Blake hesitated.

"Just one quick look," urged Dan. "No one will notice if you're late."

Blake thought a moment. "Maybe Dan's right. Mom is probably working, and Dad usually gets home late. What difference will it make that I said 4:30?"

"Okay. But only a minute," he answered.

Half an hour later, Blake left the store and once more headed for home. Now it was truly dark. The blackness hung around him, and cold stung his cheeks. His uneasiness grew.

"Two blocks more," he thought, starting to jog again.

Soon Blake turned the corner into his own block and looked toward home. The outside light and every light in the house was on. "Uh-oh," he thought.

Now, instead of hurrying, his feet dragged. Reluctantly, Blake started up the walk. Through the window he saw Mom on the phone. Behind her, seeming to wait for what was said, stood Dad.

"I'll tell them that first it was Steve's fault, and then Dan's," thought Blake. Slowly he opened the door.

TO TALK ABOUT

▶Why do you think Blake's mother was phoning someone?

▶Whose fault was it that Blake was late?

▶When did Blake make his most important choice about what time he was going to get home?

▶What difference did it make whether Blake got home at 4:30, especially if his parents weren't there?

▶Can you think of a time when you disobeyed your parents and didn't keep a promise? What choices do you wish you could change now?

"Children, obey your parents in the Lord, for this is right. 'Honor your father and mother'—which is the first commandment with a promise."
(Ephesians 6:1-2)

Lord, so often I want to do what I want to do. Sometimes it gets in the way of what my parents want of me. Help me to honor my folks by thinking about their feelings and by keeping my promises to them.

TWO CHOICES

All afternoon the sand had been warm. Bright sunlight touched the Minnesota lake with a thousand sparkles. It had been fun to meet new friends at Bible camp, but tomorrow it would all end.

Now a haze covered the sun. Sara shivered. Her swimsuit was damp and her fingernails blue from the cold. She stood up to go change her clothes, then heard Jim call her name.

"Hey, Sara, want to go for a boat ride?"

"Just a minute," she answered. "I'll change into jeans and be right back."

Once inside her cabin, Sara heard a muffled sound from a back room. She paused, and heard the noise again. Was someone crying?

Quietly Sara followed the sound to the bedroom. There she found Teresa lying face down, weeping into her pillow.

"What should I do?" Sara wondered. "Pretend I don't see? Or ask what's wrong?" She wanted to change quickly and go back to the fun. Yet as she stood there, Teresa's sobs shook the bed.

For a moment longer Sara hesitated. She hated scenes. She had been part of too many of them at home. Besides, Jim was waiting. Inside, Sara felt a tug of war begin.

Just then Teresa blew her nose. In spite of herself, Sara stepped forward. "Hey, what's wrong? Can I help?"

As Teresa looked up, her shoulders stopped shaking, but then her face disappeared into the pillow once more. Seeing Teresa's red, swollen eyes forced Sara to think back. As though seeing herself on a video screen, Sara remembered the times she'd fallen asleep crying.

Still feeling torn, yet knowing she'd hate herself if she didn't stay, Sara sat down on the bed. From somewhere came the courage to try to help. "Did you get bad news about your dad?"

Without lifting her face, Teresa shook her head.

"Then what's wrong?"

Turning her head slightly, Teresa spoke between

sniffs. "Oh, Sara, I'm scared. This week has been so perfect, I don't want to go home. It's terrible watching my dad get sicker every day. I'm scared he's going to die. What would I do without him?"

Her words ended in a sob. Sara felt helpless, unable to think of anything to say. Teresa's sobs increased.

"Help!" thought Sara. "Where can I find a counselor?" She stood up, ready to look for one.

"Don't leave," said Teresa. "Please don't go."

Sara sat down again, wanting to escape, wanting the boat ride, and feeling like a kitten stranded high in a tree. "Oh, God, how can I help her?" she prayed. "What can I say?"

In that moment words came into Sara's mind, and they didn't seem like her own. She stumbled over them, but the words came out. "Teresa, if it happens, you'll still have a Father."

"Do you mean my dad will live forever?"

Sara's hands were clammy now. She was afraid she'd say something that sounded as though she didn't care. "I mean you can still have a heavenly Father."

"Oh, God, you mean. What difference will that make?"

Sara uncurled her tense fingers. "All the difference in the world. He doesn't save us from every bad thing that happens, but He promises to be with us."

"How do you know He will? Your dad isn't dying." Teresa sat up. Her voice sounded resentful, yet her gaze clung to Sara's.

"No, but my parents are divorced. Dad lives way across the country, and I only see him one month a year."

Sara stopped. Now *she* wanted to cry. "What's happened to me is different from what's happening to you. But when Dad left . . ." she swallowed, and then went on. "When it was really hard, I found out how much I need Jesus."

Teresa's eyes seemed to brighten just a little. "Sara, how can I know Jesus the way you're talking about? I mean, *really* know Him?"

Sara's feeling of wanting to cry changed to panic. Once more she silently prayed. "What do I say now, Lord? I don't know how to explain."

Then Sara remembered last night, and Pastor Bob's talk about John 3:16. "That's one verse I know," she thought. Aloud Sara asked, "Teresa, do you know John 3:16?"

Teresa nodded. "Welllll, kind of."

"Let's see if we can say it together."

Their voices blended into one. "For God loved the world so much that he gave his only Son, so that everyone who believes in him may not die, but have eternal life."

"Teresa, do you believe Jesus died for your sins?"

"That's what Pastor Bob asked, isn't it? But it doesn't seem real to me. I have a hard time believing God can take care of me, especially if Dad dies. Is that a sin—that I don't trust God? That I don't think He's big enough?"

For a moment Teresa was quiet. "Maybe that's what keeps me from God. I *need* the love of Jesus so much, and yet I'm so scared. . . ."

Once again tears welled up in her eyes. Twice she started to speak, yet was unable to get the words out.

Again Sara felt panic. She stood up to search for a tissue and started to pray. "Oh, God, I don't know what to do—what to say. I can't answer her questions. . . ."

She found the tissue and sat down next to Teresa. In that moment Sara remembered what Pastor Bob said next.

"Teresa, I'm not smart enough to answer all your questions. But Pastor Bob said something else—that we won't always know what's going to happen to us, or if we'll be okay. But asking for salvation is taking the first step in learning to trust Jesus."

Sara still felt scared, but she cleared her throat, afraid to say, "Teresa, do you want to ask Jesus to come into your heart?"

Teresa blew her nose. The moment that she thought about it seemed to last forever. Then she nodded. "Tell me what to pray."

Quietly, sentence by sentence, Sara led Teresa.

"Jesus, I'm sorry for my sins. Thanks for dying on the cross to take them away. Please forgive me. I ask You to be my Savior. I ask You to be Lord over every part of my life—even the part of me that's scared. Thank You, Jesus, for Your salvation. Amen."

Teresa looked up. For the first time all week a light came into her eyes. "It's true. God really loves me!"

Sara hugged her. "Oh, God," she thought. "What if I'd sneaked out instead of talking to her? Oh, God, thank You!"

TO TALK ABOUT

▶What choice did Sara make when she heard Teresa crying?

▶What choice did Teresa make about her relationship with Jesus?

▶Will all of Teresa's problems be over? How will Jesus help her deal with her problems?

▶Do you know for sure that Jesus is your Savior and Lord? What choice do you need to make? To say Teresa's prayer? If so, think about that prayer, and repeat it now.

▶Or do you need to say Sara's prayer for help in telling someone about Jesus?

In your hearts set apart Christ as Lord. Always be prepared to give an answer to everyone who asks you to give the reason for the hope that you have.
(1 Peter 3:15)

Jesus, I want to set You apart as Savior and Lord. Help me to always be prepared to talk with anyone who asks about the salvation You've given me.

ANYA'S DREAM

Anya's workout time that morning had been shot through with glory. Though there were no windows, it seemed that sunlight washed the gym. When she came down off the uneven parallel bars, her gymnastics coach had cheered her on. "You've got it, Anya!"

Now she was back after school, making sure of every part of her routine. She wanted nothing to distract her from the perfection she'd like to achieve.

With a flying run Anya grabbed hold of the uneven parallel bar. Up, over, beat, twist. As she worked out, she sensed rather than saw that people had stopped and turned to watch. Yet she kept on, sure in her timing, holding her concentration. If she won at the meet tomorrow, who knows how far she could go.

With a final twist, Anya was on the mat, arms stretched high above her head, her spirit soaring.

The applause came. "Perfect, Anya! Absolutely perfect!" called her coach. "Now take a break. Go home and get a good night's sleep. You're ready for the meet tomorrow."

She knew he was right. She was tired, yet. . . . "Just one more time," she answered.

Taking her first position, Anya poised her body, letting the routine go through her mind. Then she took a deep breath.

The run came easy. She reached out, grabbed the bar, swung up into a handstand. Down, under, swing, reach.

"Not quite right," Anya told herself. Somehow her timing was off, and she fought to recover. Up, over, beat, reach. . . .

The next moment Anya felt the floor coming up. Instinctively she reached out, and her left hand took the fall. Pain shot through her arm, sucked down like a giant wave, and washed over her body. Then her world went black.

Several hours later, Anya looked up from a hospital bed. She seemed surrounded by bright light. Her mom stood at the side of the bed, her coach nearby.

"Have they been crying?" wondered Anya to herself. "Coach Sanders wouldn't. He'd never cry." She

drifted off again, then came back.

"I don't like the look on their faces," she thought. But her eyes felt weighted. She couldn't seem to keep a thought in her mind. Again she drifted off, then opened her eyes. "Have *I* been crying?" she wondered. "What's wrong?"

Then Anya felt the cast on her hand and arm, and the shock went through her. "I don't want to ask," she thought. "If I don't ask, maybe it won't be true." She pushed the question to the back of her mind, trying to avoid it.

But she couldn't avoid her mother's eyes. Mom reached out and pushed the hair back from Anya's forehead. "Take it easy, Annie. I love you," she said.

"Annie!" Anya felt sick all through. "Mom hasn't called me Annie since I was a little kid. That's what she called me when she put me on her lap, and washed my scraped knees, and kissed the bandages. . . ."

No longer could she escape the question. "What happened?" she said aloud.

Sanders took her good hand. "Sorry, Anya. I saw you going, and I couldn't reach you fast enough. . . ."

"It's bad," thought Anya. "Really bad." But she couldn't quite take it in yet. Her eyes felt too heavy.

Anya drifted off to sleep, but in the days ahead, she came wide awake. As she left the hospital and returned to the apartment where she and her mother lived, Anya had no choice but to face what had happened. A broken wrist. Not just one bone, but two had been shattered and crushed. Yes, a specialist had operated on it. Yes, he had done all he could. But. . . .

With every waking moment Anya felt questions gnaw inside her. "Will I be able to work on the uneven parallel bars again? Will my wrist be strong enough for handstands? Will I ever compete again?"

At night the questions haunted her, questions she was afraid to ask, until one day she knew she must.

Her doctor shook his head. "I don't know, Anya. I wish I could tell you something different. Yet it would be worse if I said everything is going to be okay. One day you might find out I lied to you. I have to be honest in telling you it's the worst break I've seen, and I've seen a lot."

He didn't have to say more. Anya remembered her mom's expression when she woke up. She remembered how Sanders had looked. She couldn't escape what she had seen in their eyes.

"It can't be true, God, can it? You wouldn't let this happen."

It had been a long time since Anya talked with God, but now she had plenty to tell Him. "You're supposed to be a God of love. How can You do this to me?" Each morning she woke up, wanting to shake her fist at God, wanting to cry out.

One day when her mom was gone from their

apartment, Anya shouted her rage. "God, I wanted to be a champion gymnast! How can You wreck my life this way?"

The sound seemed to bounce back at her. The apartment walls closed in around her, but the questions would not stop. "Why, God, why? Why *me*?"

In the silence that came, there were no answers. The silence seemed to bleed with Anya's pain.

The next morning she got up early, the way she used to. Every day she went into the gym and watched the others work out. More than once her coach tried to get her off the bench.

"Come on, Anya," he said. "Come over here and give tips to the others. Tell them how to improve."

Each time Anya shook her head, telling herself, "He's just trying to make me feel better. I'm not really needed." Then a deeper thought plagued her. "If I can't be a gymnast anymore, why should I help someone else?"

As the days went on, Anya's anger deepened and her despair grew. Then one morning her coach found her outside the gym, trying to hide her tears. This time Sanders made no request for help. His voice was soft, but there was steel running through it. "Anya, I taught you to be a champion. You're not acting like one." Abruptly he turned and went back into the gym.

Anya fled, afraid to face her own feelings. "I don't have to go back," she told herself. "I'll just stay away."

But that night she had a dream. Anya saw herself poised, standing ready for her routine. As she started to run, her feet bit into the floor. Faster, faster. Grab the bar. Up, over, under, twist. Reach out, up a perfect handstand. Down, under, up. Another flip. Then her feet hit the mat. Standing with upstretched arms, she waited for the applause. It thundered around her.

Anya woke up crying. She pulled the blanket over her head. Cushioning her left wrist with her pillow, she cried until her body shook. "It's in me, isn't it, God? Will I always want to be a gymnast?"

Anya didn't know the answer, but suddenly she felt a stillness within. Something inside had changed.

Pushing back the blankets, Anya dressed, said goodbye to Mom, and started for the gym. As she opened its door, she made her decision. "Okay, God. If I can't be a champion gymnast, I'll be the best coach there ever was."

With her head high, Anya walked over and stood near the uneven parallel bars. When she decided something, Anya meant it.

TO TALK ABOUT

▶ Why was Anya afraid to face the fact that her wrist was broken?

▶ After something difficult happens, people often feel angry with God. What happened when Anya went beyond being angry *at* God and started talking *with* Him about her feelings?

▶ How did Anya choose between feeling sorry for herself and going on with her life?

▶ When it becomes impossible to reach a goal, it often helps to substitute something similar. As Anya works toward a new goal, what achievements might make her happy?

▶ It's good to have dreams about accomplishing something worthwhile if we keep those dreams in balance and don't allow them to control us. How had Anya's dream of being a gymnast started to control her?

▶ God can give us dreams about what we are supposed to be in life. If you don't have such a dream, why is it important to ask God for one?

▶ Why is it important to work toward a goal, even if we don't always achieve everything we hope for? What are some of the dreams you're working toward?

I have learned to be content whatever the circumstances. (Philippians 4:11)

It's hard to be happy, to be content, Lord, if things aren't going the way I want. Help me to turn away from feeling sorry for myself and be what You want me to be. Give me a big dream, God, about how You want to use my life. Then show me how to reach the goals You give me.

IF YOU SNITCH I'LL...

"Come on, Scott."

"Where do you wanna go?"

"There's not much time. I'll show you."

Scott dropped his books into his locker and followed his friend Mitch down the hall. A moment later they were outside, and the brisk wind felt good after being in school all day.

"Where're we going?" he asked again.

"I'm meeting some kids at a house down the street. Have to be there in five minutes. They'll leave if I'm not on time. Come on."

The urgency in his voice sparked Scott's interest. Mitch took off, his long legs stretching out into a hurried stride. Scott had all he could do to keep up.

A block later Mitch slowed his pace, looked up and down the street, and turned onto a narrow path leading to a house. Scott was out of breath, but struggled to speak. "What's going on? Who lives here?"

"Never mind. You're my friend, and I just want you with me," answered Mitch as he knocked on a side door.

A split second later the door opened as if by magic. Scott could see no one, but Mitch stepped inside. As Scott hesitated, Mitch reached back and pulled him in. "Come *on*," said Mitch sharply. "I told you to move."

Scott stood with his back to the door while his eyes adjusted to the change of light. In the dim kitchen, he saw Mitch reach out for a small packet. A moment later it disappeared. Then Scott and Mitch were outside again. As Mitch reached the street, he looked both ways, up and down the sidewalk, then started back toward school.

"Now, will you tell me what that was all about?" demanded Scott.

"Sure, sure, you're in on it now. Got some for you to try."

"Got some *what*?" Slowly light dawned on Scott, and he stopped deadstill in the middle of the sidewalk. "Mitch, do you mean. . . ." The full understanding of what they had just done staggered him. "Mitch, do you mean *drugs*? You're doing drugs? But we agreed! We promised each other!"

"We promised each other we would always do things together. That's what being friends is, isn't it? So I brought you along. I want you to give it a try."

"Hey, Mitch, that promise didn't mean we should do something wrong together. Drugs will hurt us!"

"Are you sure? Is that what your parents say? How do you know if you haven't tried? I want to find out for myself. Some kids say. . . ."

"I don't wanna listen to you," Scott snapped. "You're thinking crazy! Have you already tried some?"

"Wellllll," Mitch looked down, and kicked his toe against the edge of the curb.

"Well, I'm not going with you on this one," said Scott.

"Aw, come on, we're friends," answered Mitch. "You can't do that to me. I let you in on something good."

"Something bad, you mean. I'm not part of this one."

"Oh yes you are! You went to the house. You're in it too. If I get caught, I'll tell people you took me there."

Scott's stomach bottomed out. He *was* part of it. He had stood there watching Mitch take the packet. He hadn't said a word. "What can I do?" he asked himself, feeling desperate.

"And don't you dare snitch," said Mitch. "If you squeal, I'll beat you up!"

"Beat me up?" Scott felt scared. He felt like a

million motorcycles were circling a track in his brain. They seemed to make so much noise he couldn't think straight.

"I'm not a snitch," he thought. "I hate it when kids squeal on others. But is this the same? Not tell *anyone*? Not even Mom or Dad? What if Mitch gets hooked?"

In that moment the motorcycles stopped. Scott's head cleared. "If Mitch gets hooked, would it be my fault because I didn't say anything?" he asked himself.

"Promise you won't snitch on me," demanded Mitch. "I mean it. I'll beat you up!"

Inside Scott the motorcycles started again. Again his feelings were mixed up, and his tongue felt as if it wouldn't move. Then the words came. "I promise. . . ." He stopped. "No, I don't."

For an instant Scott stood there. Then he ducked out of Mitch's reach. Knowing they'd probably never be friends again, Scott started for home on a run.

TO TALK ABOUT

▶What do you feel Scott should do—tell his parents about Mitch and what he's doing, or keep quiet?
▶What is the difference between being a snitch and telling a responsible person about something that may hurt someone?
▶If Scott continues to say no to drugs, what will

happen to his friendship with Mitch?
▶ Is a friendship worth keeping at any cost?

Flee the evil desires of youth, and pursue righteous-
ness, faith, love and peace, along with those who
call on the Lord out of a pure heart (2 Timothy 2:22)

Lord, help me to run away from doing wrong things.
Give me the power of Your Holy Spirit to say no in
such a way that kids know I mean it, and leave me
alone. Give me courage, too, so that someone's life
isn't harmed because I'm afraid to speak to the right
person at the right time. Help me, Jesus. I really need
You.

127

HOME, SWEET HOME

Annie gazed out the school bus window at the farms they passed. Houses glistened in the autumn sun. Silos stood tall. Cows and horses grazed quietly.

Annie felt as if she were seeing them for the first time. She sneaked a look at Tricia, wondering how her friend from school would like her house and family. "I was crazy to invite her home," Annie thought, as nervous jiggles bounced around in her stomach. "Whatever made me do it?"

As though she could hear Annie's thoughts, Tricia spoke. "I've always wanted to visit you."

Then Annie remembered how this had come about. Tricia had practically invited herself! Would

she be disappointed in what she saw? Would she like
Randy and Sue, who were sitting in the back of the
bus with the older kids? What would she think of the
room Annie shared with four-year-old Dawn?

All around Annie kids talked about what happened at school that day. But Annie was quiet, thinking back to her visit to Tricia's. What a room she had!
A canopy bed with a flouncy spread. Her own record
player. Stuffed animals all over the room. And a beautiful, big, quiet house. No brothers or sisters to fight
with or mess things up.

Brakes squealed, and the bus ground to a halt.
Silently Annie began to pray. "I'm scared, Lord. I don't
know if I can handle it if Tricia doesn't like our place.
What if she even tells me so, the way she does when
she doesn't like something at school? You take care of
it, Jesus, will You?"

Out of long habit Annie stood up, clutched her
lunch box and sweater, and followed Sue and Randy
down the steps. Tricia trailed behind.

"At least our driveway isn't muddy right now,"
thought Annie.

As always, Dawn stood at the door, waiting for
Annie, Sue, and Randy to come home. Annie tousled
her hair. "Hi, Kitten. This is Tricia."

Tricia stopped to look into the little girl's face.
"How old are you?" she asked.

Dawn held up four fingers. "Next year I go to

school!" She tucked her hand in Annie's. "I made cookies for you today."

Annie grinned, knowing Dawn must have had quite a bit of help from Mom. The fragrance of freshly baked cookies still lingered in the air. Annie walked into the kitchen and introduced Tricia just as Mom poured large glasses of milk.

Mom's smile was as warm as the kitchen. "So far, so good," thought Annie as she and Tricia joined Sue and Randy at the table. But five minutes later Randy rolled his eyeballs heavenward and smirked at Sue.

"Stop it!" cried Sue. Underneath the table her foot came down hard on Randy's toes.

He jumped up, shaking his foot, as he limped around the table. "Ow, ow, ow! You do too like him! Say you do," he insisted.

"*Randy.*" Mom's voice held a warning.

Sue's face was red and her eyes bright with unshed tears. "Be quiet, Randy," she muttered.

"I saw you looking at him. I saw you passing a note on the bus," he teased.

Sue stood up, set her glass down hard, and ran blindly to her room.

Annie wanted to crawl under a chair. Once again she sneaked a look at her friend. Tricia had a quiet smile on her face. She seemed just plain interested. How could anyone be interested in watching a brother and sister fight?

Slowly Annie pushed back her chair. "Well, I guess I better get it over with," she thought. "I wonder how Tricia will like my room."

Moments later Tricia stood at the door. As she looked around, Annie watched her. Tricia's gaze stopped on the second bed. "Dawn sleeps here?" she asked. "You get to talk at night whenever you want?"

Slowly Annie nodded. "What is Tricia thinking?" she wondered.

TO TALK ABOUT

▶How do you think Tricia feels about Annie's room and her family?

▶How can you choose to like where you live, even though it's different from someone else's home? What happens if you concentrate on the good things about your home and family?

▶God wants families to offer love and a sense of caring about each other. What other qualities make us feel like a home is a good place to be?

▶What matters most—the material things in a home or the love and support of the people living there?

▶If Annie lived in a home where she didn't get that love and support, how could knowing God help her?

▶In what ways is it important to pray for your family? What are some things you can ask God to do?

Keep me from paying attention to what is worthless;
be good to me, as you have promised.
(Psalm 119:37, GNB)

Jesus, when I keep thinking about what other kids
have, that's paying attention to something that's
worthless, isn't it? Thanks that no matter what my
family's like, we aren't perfect. Thanks that some-
times I can do something to improve the way things
are. But thanks most of all that this is where I belong.
Give me Your big love for every person in my family.

TONI MAKES A DISCOVERY

Toni felt nervous as she entered the long hallway. Since moving to a new school, she'd dreaded Monday mornings. It seemed everyone had plenty to talk about. Everyone had a special friend. Everyone belonged to a group.

"Everyone, that is, except me," thought Toni.

Already a cluster of girls had formed around Dena's locker. Toni knew they'd be talking about all that had happened that weekend. She wished she could join them. It'd be fun to listen, even if she didn't have much to say.

At the same time Toni felt afraid to walk past them. They all seemed very sure of themselves and often made her feel shut out. Yet her locker was a short way down the hall beyond Dena's.

"Maybe someone will notice my new blouse," thought Toni, remembering how great she'd looked that morning. "Maybe they'll think I'm worth having in their group." A tiny spark of hope came to life. "There's Janet. Janet knows me. She'll say hi."

Trying to look more confident than she felt, Toni drew a deep breath. "If I smile, they have to smile back." But even as the thought came, she started feeling shaky inside.

As Toni neared the girls, Janet looked up. Toni stopped. "Hi, Janet," she said, the words feeling stiff on her lips.

For a moment she thought Janet would answer. Instead, she raised her chin slightly and turned back to the others. All the girls laughed.

Toni felt the hot flood of embarrassment surge to her face. She wanted to run, yet seemed frozen to the spot. Somehow she put one foot in front of another. "Were they laughing at me?" she wondered. "Or just trying to make me feel left out?"

Either way, Toni knew it made no difference. Instead of going to her locker, she headed for the bathroom.

To her relief it was empty. She'd been spending a lot of time there. She knew every crack in the floor, every faucet that didn't quite turn off. She wished she could hide there forever.

Dropping her books on a ledge, Toni went to the mirror. Somehow her new blouse didn't seem nearly as nice as it had earlier that day. She felt the soft material and tried to believe it was still important. It wasn't. Instead, the mirror reflected the tears glistening in her brown eyes.

Toni blinked those tears away, but her lips trembled. "I'm not going to cry," she told herself. The loneliness she felt was too deep. On the days like this it seemed the ache would never go away. "It's no use. They'll never accept me. I'll never be part of their group."

It wasn't the first time Toni had prayed, but now she meant business. "Jesus, help me. I don't know what to do. I forgive them, but I feel worthless. I need friends."

In that moment the warning bell rang. Toni picked up her books and walked out slowly, dreading the hours ahead.

The days passed, and Toni wondered if God would answer her prayer. Nothing seemed to change. The girls who gathered at Dena's locker still laughed or looked away when she passed. Toni pasted a smile on her face, but she no longer tried to say hi. She knew it was no use.

Yet one Monday when Toni walked past the girls, she had the strangest feeling—as though she didn't walk alone.

Not quite sure what had happened, Toni thought about it. "Nothing's changed." Then she realized that wasn't quite true. "I forgave them, didn't I? Is that what made the difference?"

As she stood by her locker, Toni tried to figure it out. "It felt like an invisible bubble around me. Their meanness didn't get through."

In that moment she remembered Jesus and His long walk to the cross. She knew who had walked with her.

For the first time Toni saw the girls as they were. Her thoughts exploded. "I don't *need* a bunch of stuck-up friends! I don't *need* kids who just think about clothes!"

In that instant Toni felt like a different person. She knew she'd made a big discovery. "It's *their* problem, not mine!"

She wanted to shout it to the whole world. "Wow! Why'd it take me so long to figure that out?"

Then she had another thought. "If that's the way they treat me, what do they do to other kids? Are they mean to everyone outside their group?"

It didn't take long to find out. On Wednesday a new girl named Karla started school. Dena and her friends gave Karla the same treatment.

But now Toni knew what she could do, and she felt good about trying. "I'll start by making friends with Karla."

TO TALK ABOUT

▶Sometimes kids feel they can show power by shutting other kids out. How was Toni shut out by the in-group? What do you think of a group that treats someone that way?

▶How does it feel to be shut out? Can you think of a time when you were shut out or when you shut out someone else? What happened?

▶When we need to forgive someone, we don't have to wait until we feel good about them or like what they're doing. Toni forgave Dena's group with her will by praying, "Jesus, I forgive them." After her prayer, what changes did God bring?

▶What discovery helped Toni find a way out of her unhappiness? Does her discovery help you in a similar situation?

▶Why does Jesus understand when we feel lonely and rejected? How do you know? For clues read Isaiah 53, a chapter that tells what would happen to Jesus hundreds of years later.

▶God always hears our prayers. Yet He may not suddenly make everything right in the way we hope. Instead, He may give us a sense of being loved, or change how we feel about what's happening. Have you felt Jesus with you in one of those ways? Has He helped you accept something hard, even though you didn't like it? What happened?

▶How do you know Jesus loves you, even if you can't "feel" that He does?

Jesus said, "I will never turn away anyone who comes to me." (John 6:37, GNB)

Jesus, I don't like feeling lonely and left out. But I forgive the kids who make me feel that way. I'm glad You will never reject me. Thanks for always loving me. Help me know deep inside that You do.

140

YOU WANT TO
BE A WHAT?

Troy pushed his books to one side of his desk as Mrs. Irving stood to introduce the day's speaker. Each week the teacher had invited someone to talk about a career possibility. "Today it's our pleasure to have with us Dr. Kent Simpson," she said.

The class clapped politely, but Troy leaned forward, not wanting to miss a word.

"Thanks for inviting me," Dr. Simpson began. "I want to tell you why I decided to become a doctor."

As Troy listened, he felt he had wakened to find a dream come true. Everything Dr. Simpson talked about sounded exactly like what he wanted to do—except for one thing. Troy wanted to be a doctor in

Africa, or in another Third-World country.

Soon Dr. Simpson finished speaking and left. Troy's teacher cleared her throat. "I've been reading the papers you wrote to tell me what career you're considering. Troy, your paper entitled 'Why I'd Like to Be a Missionary Doctor' is excellent. I want everyone to hear it. You understand how people feel. You'll make an excellent doctor."

Troy felt as if cold sweat were rolling down his spine. "I understand how people think all right," he mumbled to himself. "Now it'll start all over again—the teasing, the name calling. . . ." He wished he could smear on vanishing cream.

As Mrs. Irving began reading his paper, Troy looked down, avoiding the wink of the boy across the aisle. Soon Bryce passed Troy a note: "Help me, Doc! I scratched my arm."

Troy stared straight ahead. "Why can't Mrs. Irving tell them I'm a good ball player?" he wondered.

The teacher kept reading: "I would like to use my training as a doctor to become a missionary. . . ."

Just then Josie, the girl in front of Troy, turned around, smiled shyly, and turned back. The rustling in the room grew quiet. Now everyone listened. Troy knew they were collecting more ways to make fun of him.

Finally Mrs. Irving finished. "Pssssst," whispered Bryce.

Troy pretended not to hear.

"Hey, preacher man," said Bryce in a louder whisper. This time those around him turned to hear more. "How can I get to Heaven?"

Two boys snickered. "All I want to do is get out of here," thought Troy. "I'll never write another paper telling what I *really* think."

At last the day ended, and Troy escaped outside. Questions flew at him like missiles. "Why do you want to go to a place like that?" asked one girl. "It's much more fun around here."

A boy joined in. "Sure, be a doctor in the United States. You'd make big bucks. But a missionary? You gotta be kidding."

As soon as he could, Troy left the others and started home. "I feel like I'm the only one who wants to do something with my life. How come I want what other kids *don't* want?"

Faster and faster Troy walked, and his thoughts kept pace with his steps. "Why doesn't something count unless I make lots of money doing it? Do I *really* want to help people by being a missionary doctor? Are the kids right, Lord? What about it, are they right?"

In the midst of the sidewalk he stopped for a moment, knowing the answer to his question would change his life. Then he straightened his shoulders and went on, feeling the weight of his decision fall off. For the first time all afternoon, he felt peaceful.

A smile spread across his face. "Or do I know something the other kids don't know?"

TO TALK ABOUT

▶When kids tease, does it always mean they don't like the person they make fun of? Why might kids tease someone they secretly respect?

▶Would the others tease Troy less if he thought of a funny way to answer them? What might he say?

▶Troy thinks he's the only one who wants to do something with his life. Why is it possible that he's not being realistic in how he feels? What clue hints at what Josie believes?

▶It's important for each of us to know the way in which God calls us. Do you think Troy should keep his goal of becoming a missionary doctor?

▶What do you think of a value system that chooses a career simply on the basis of making money?

▶How would you answer Troy's final question?

Am I now trying to win the approval of men, or of God? Or am I trying to please men? If I were still trying to please men, I could not be a servant of Christ. (Galatians 1:10)

Jesus, forgive me when my desire to be liked gets in the way of being the person You want me to be. Help me to be a friend to others, but also to keep my eyes on whatever goals You give me. Someday I want to serve You in the career I enter. Help me prepare through the things I learn now.

GIFT FROM A GRANDMA

Skates glistening in the afternoon sun, Tammy spun like a top, her long braid flying out from the back of her head. As she twirled to a stop, her friends from school clapped.

Jay's eyes shone in admiration. "You did it, Tammy! Good for you!"

"You didn't even wobble," added Cheryl.

Tammy felt the warm flush of being praised spread across her cheeks. It felt good to do something well, and the crisp afternoon air gave the day a special brightness. Around her, the pond was filled with skaters, some sure of themselves, others moving uncertainly. Tammy wished the day could go on forever.

"Hey, you know what would be fun?" asked Cheryl. "Let's have a skating party tomorrow night."

"Sounds good," said Jay. "It's the only night this week they'll have the lights on."

Happiness welled up inside Tammy. "That's a great idea! Jay, why don't you ask the boys, and Cheryl and I can ask the girls, and. . . . Oh, no!"

"What's the matter?" asked Jay.

Tammy made a face. "The kids at church are going to a nursing home tomorrow night. We're supposed to sing Christmas carols and talk to people."

"Oh, Tammy," said Cheryl. "Can't you skip it? It would be so much more fun to be here."

"I know," said Tammy. She thought about being cooped up inside stuffy halls and then about how much she liked to skate. Besides, Jay would be here, and of all the boys at school, Jay was the nicest.

"No one will ever know if you skip the singing," said Cheryl.

"Maybe you're right," said Tammy slowly. Suddenly she made a quick turn on the ice. She knew she was only trying to fool herself.

She scraped to a halt. "What if everyone thinks the same thing? What if no one shows up?"

She looked at Jay, wishing his face would tell her what to do, but it didn't. "You have the party anyway," she said.

Tammy knew her words were right, but the next

evening she still felt empty about not being with her friends. Going up the steps of the nursing home, she couldn't help but think of the party. Yet she looked around the small caroling group and knew she was needed.

Warm air greeted them as they started down the hall. "Joy to the world! The Lord is come. . . ." Tammy sang as loud as she could, yet wondered what Jay and Cheryl and the others were doing.

A heavily decorated tree stood in the middle of the large room they entered. Its soft lights cast a glow on the people gathered around. "Away in a manger, no crib for His bed, the little Lord Jesus laid down His sweet head. . . ."

In that moment all thoughts of the skating party vanished, for Tammy caught sight of a little white-haired lady sitting in a wheelchair. Dressed in her Sunday best, her hands folded in her lap, her gaze clung to the faces of the singers. Quietly, as though she didn't know what was happening, a tear started down her cheek.

When they finished singing, Tammy went to her. "I'm Tammy," she said. "You remind me of my grandmother who died last year."

"And you look like my granddaughter who lives far away," said the little lady. "Call me Grandma Ruth if you like." Her smile was like the sun coming out from beneath a cloud.

Soon it was time for Tammy to go. Grandma Ruth reached forward to tuck something into her hand. "Thank you," she said. "Thank you for bringing Christmas to me."

Looking down, Tammy saw a fine white handkerchief with beautiful lace around the edge. She knew the little woman had used it to dry her tears.

Grandma Ruth smiled. "I love you," she said.

Now it was Tammy's turn to blink away tears. "I love *you*," she answered, as though she were talking to her own grandmother. She leaned forward for a quick hug, surprised at how much her new friend meant to her. Then she turned and hurried with the others to the car.

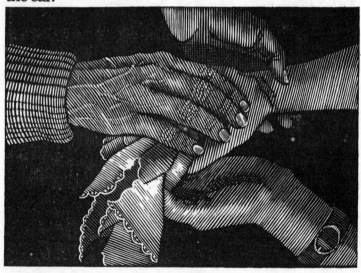

For the first time since entering the building, Tammy remembered the skating party. Yet she felt no regret. She knew she'd made the right choice.

Quietly she started humming. "Should I go back to see her again?" she asked herself. "I think I know."

TO TALK ABOUT

▶Why was Tammy's choice especially hard to make?
▶If Jay is as nice as Tammy thinks, what do you suppose he thought about her because she went to the nursing home?
▶Why do visitors mean so much to people in a nursing home?
▶What did Tammy receive that was better than a handkerchief?

"Give, and it will be given to you. . . . For with the measure you use, it will be measured to you."
(Luke 6:38)

It's really hard, Lord, when I have to choose between something that's fun and something that helps others. Help me to put the most important things first. Help me to love lonely people the way You love me.

IS IT WORTH THE FIGHT?

Nick wasn't sure where it all started. Maybe it began with the emptiness he felt inside. Or was it because he ached with wanting a dad or mom who really cared about what happened to him?

But Nick remembered the day Kevin said, "Our church has a gym where we can shoot baskets. Want to stop off on the way home from school?"

There Nick surprised even himself. As the ball swished through the net, Kevin called out, "Hey, good shot! Keep it up!" Warmed by Kevin's praise, Nick kept on being a winner. Time after time he darted under the net, retrieved the ball, then charged in again.

A few weeks later Kevin asked, "Want to go to

Sunday school with me? You'll like our teacher. He talks about things that are real."

Nick wasn't sure about that. It was one thing to shoot baskets, another to go to church. And Sunday school? After all, hadn't his mom said that Sunday school was just for sissies? And church for those people not smart enough to make it on their own?

Over several weeks Kevin kept asking. Finally Nick said yes, but once he got there he wasn't sure he was in the right place. "I'd like to hide in a corner," he thought.

Yet Kevin's teacher wouldn't let him. He kept drawing Nick into the conversation. "Today we're going to talk about Gideon," he said.

Kevin opened a book Nick had never seen and helped him find the place. "Think of something that really makes you afraid," said the teacher.

"That's not hard," thought Nick. "I'm afraid of what Mom will say when she finds out where I've been."

The teacher began reading, "But the Lord had told Gideon, 'Go in the strength you have and save Israel out of Midian's hand. Am I not sending you?' (Judges 6:14). . . ."

Nick liked the story and liked seeing Gideon win. He wanted to come back and hear more stories from the book he had never read. Yet what would Mom say?

As he opened the kitchen door, she stood by the

sink. "Where have you been?" she asked.

He tried to slip past without answering, but Mom stopped him. "Where have you been, Nick?" she repeated.

Inside, Nick felt his heart begin to pound. He braced his feet. "Out," he said.

"Out where?"

Nick swallowed hard, but finally spoke. "I went to Sunday school with Kevin."

"Sunday school?" His mom's eyes flashed. *"Sunday school?"*

"Yeah, Mom, and I liked it."

"You liked being with all those sissies and do-gooders?"

Nick tried to put on the blank-face mask he usually wore in front of his mom. Yet he couldn't seem to manage. Something else broke through, something he wanted her to know. "Yeah, Mom," he said again. "I liked the kids. They aren't sissies. Kev likes to shoot baskets. Dan plays football. And I liked the story I heard."

"I don't think much of this God stuff," said his mother. "It's all a bunch of nonsense. Just fairy tales. This is the real world."

"Hey, Mom, you've got it all wrong. . . ."

"Don't you start preaching to me, young man. Don't tell *me* what to do."

Now the pounding of Nick's heart was so strong

155

he wondered if Mom could see. He was scared of her, yet more scared of the emptiness he felt inside. He felt as if he were drowning, as though he were going down for the last time. He didn't want to talk about Sunday school. Yet if he didn't, he knew he had no hope of being with the class again.

Nick stepped back out of her reach. "I want to go back, Mom. Next Sunday I want to go back."

Mom's face flushed red. She drew a deep breath, and in the next instant her face drained of color. The iciness in her voice was terrible, worse than the angry words she usually spoke.

"Okay," she said. "But you go by yourself. You get there by yourself. Don't ever ask for a ride, even if it's cold or rainy. We'll see how long you manage to stick it out."

Abruptly she turned, and Nick knew by the way she slammed the door that the battle was just beginning.

For a long time he stood looking out the window. "Should I go back?" he asked himself. "I'll always be going alone. Is it worth the fight?"

TO TALK ABOUT

▶ What do you think Nick will decide about going to church?

▶ What possible effect could Nick's going to Sunday

school have on his mother?

▶Why are some people against going to church? What do you think about the reasons they give?

▶It's important to look at how Jesus lived while on earth, instead of always watching people. Yet how can it be helpful to us to be with other Christians and see how they live?

▶Nick does not yet know Jesus as his Savior and Lord. Why will that make it especially hard for him to keep going to Sunday school?

▶If Nick becomes a Christian, what are some ways for him to handle his mother's negative comments?

I was glad when they said to me, "Let us go to the LORD's house." (Psalm 122:1, GNB)

Jesus, my family is a lot like Nick's, and I'm afraid to tell anyone. Give me someone who will understand and help me go to church. I want to believe in You, Jesus. I want to learn more about You.

157

THIRTY MINUTES AND COUNTING

Rosita twisted her flute together and set her music rack next to the open window. A gentle breeze lifted the pages of her exercise book. She looked out.

Down the street the kids had a volleyball game going. Through the warm summer air the sounds came clearly. Rosita wished she were there.

"Mommmm!" she called. "Do I have to practice?"

Mom poked her head in the door. "Put in your half hour, and you'll be free the rest of the day."

Rosita glanced at the clock and sighed, making sure Mom heard her groan. "Why did I say I wanted to play the flute?" Rosita asked. "I must have had rocks in my head."

"No, you didn't," said Mom. "Remember how much you liked hearing that flutist at church?"

"But I didn't think it was going to be so hard."

"We bought the flute," said Mom. "Give it a fair chance. See how you feel at the end of six months."

She started to leave, then turned. "I'm going to the store in a few minutes. I'll be back in less than an hour."

Mom disappeared, and once again Rosita faced her exercise book. "A note followed by a dot has its value increased one half," she read. "Phooey!"

Tapping her foot to keep time, she began playing. One, two, three, rest. One, two, three, rest.

Next she tried her scales. G, A, B, C. . . .

Rosita stopped. The volleyball had rolled down this way. As she watched, her friend Kristy ran to pick it up, then went back to the game.

Once again Rosita blew across the hole in the mouthpiece—D, E, F, G.

She paused. "How do I hit high A?" Taking out the sheet of fingerings, Rosita stared at the circles her instructor had drawn on a paper.

Just then she heard the car leave the garage. As quickly as she could, Rosita twisted her flute apart, put it in its case, and hurried outside.

Moments later she was playing volleyball with her friends. Yet somehow Rosita didn't feel right about it. It seemed as if she had lost a different game.

All through the month of June, Rosita practiced with her music rack next to the window. She longed to be out with the kids. Always she thought of that moment when she would finish her thirty minutes.

Then one morning something inside Rosita changed. After hurrying through the scales, she opened her book of songs. As she played the notes, her mind began thinking the words. "Jingle bells, jingle bells, jingle all the way. . . ."

The tune was catchy, and she played it several times, surprised that it sounded better with each try.

Next, Rosita found "Twinkle, Twinkle, Little Star." Soon her lower lip was sore, and she felt lightheaded from blowing. But when she glanced at the clock, she discovered twenty-five minutes had passed.

That day Rosita moved her music rack away from the window. Somehow it didn't seem as important to watch the kids down the street.

The next Sunday morning the flutist was back in church. Again and again she soared to the high notes. To Rosita the sound was sweet.

"How can she do it?" she thought. Now she knew how hard it was to reach those notes. Something within her reached out, longing to play better, longing to play well. "Will you help me, God? Will you help me play like that?"

A few moments later the thrilling notes slowed. The flutist swung into a quiet melody, simply played.

161

Rosita knew the words. "In my life, Lord, be glorified, be glorified. . . ."

She wasn't ready to hear the song end. She wanted the clear high notes to last forever.

The next morning the melody was still in Rosita's mind. "I wish I could play it," she thought. She searched in her books, but couldn't find the song.

As soon as she finished her scales, she started her other music. But the song from church stayed in her mind. "In my life, Lord. . . ." As clearly as if she had just heard it, Rosita remembered the tune.

For the first time she began going up and down the scale, listening for a certain note.

"There it is," she thought. "It's E." She tried again and found the second note. Now she felt excited. E, G, E, G. As she stumbled around, she picked out the rest of the tune. Over and over she played it, afraid she would forget the notes.

Just then Rosita glanced at the clock. She had gone five minutes over!

A smile welled up from within her, a smile of surprise. For the first time it had been fun to play the flute.

TO TALK ABOUT

▶When Rosita found it hard to practice, what poor choice did she make? Can you remember times when you did something similar? What happened?

▶ How do you think Rosita would have felt about herself if she had given up when she found it hard to practice? Why?

▶ For most people learning to play an instrument is hard work until they reach a breakthrough. What good choices helped Rosita come to the breakthrough where she *liked* playing the flute?

▶ Often we think of a reward as some good outward thing that happens to us. A reward can also come in the way we feel inside. How did Rosita experience a reward in both ways?

▶ If we pray about learning how to play an instrument, does that mean we can stop practicing? How do you know?

▶ What are some skills you've had to work hard to learn? If you choose to learn something new, how does it make a difference in the way you feel about yourself?

Surely you will reward each person according to what he has done. (Psalm 62:12)

Jesus, I don't like to practice or work at learning something. In those times help me to keep going. Thank You that when You help me learn, I see how big You are, and feel good about the way You made me. Help me remember that my abilities are gifts from You.

LYING TO MYSELF

It took only a moment, and it was done. "I want to come home later tonight," said Jackie. "I'd like to go to Debbie's after school."

Mom looked her straight in the eyes. "You'll be at Debbie's? And you'll be home by 5:30?"

For a split second Jackie hesitated. Yet when she said it, the lie seemed easy. "Sure, Mom, at Debbie's. I'll be home at 5:30. Just in time for supper."

Avoiding Mom's eyes, Jackie gave her a hug, and moments later was out the door. As the below-freezing air hit her face, her cheeks began to tingle. Squinting her eyes against the glistening white snow, Jackie started the four long blocks to school.

Halfway there she met Margaret. "Can you come,

Jackie?" she asked. "The boys said they could."

"Sure, I'll see you after school. Mom didn't catch on. I told her I'm going to Debbie's."

Hours later Jackie reached Margaret's front door. Bart and Tim were already there and a strong bass thumped from the boom box. For a moment Jackie felt a twinge of uneasiness. It was as though she heard another tape, one of Mom saying, "You can't go to Margaret's after school. I don't want you there, especially when her mother is at work."

"Yeah, Mom, yeah," Jackie had promised. Now she pushed down the twinge. "Mom will never know," she told herself. "I can take care of myself. I know how to handle older boys."

Turning on her brightest smile, Jackie entered the living room. Over in the corner Bart stood up. "Hi, Jackie," he said.

Just the way he said it make Jackie feel uncomfortable. Immediately she pushed the feeling down. Soon she slipped into the beat of the music and forgot the whispers of her conscience. "Sure is more fun dancing with Bart than being at Debbie's," she thought.

But Bart kept pressing closer. Each time Jackie moved back he stepped forward. "I should like this," thought Jackie. "Instead, I feel like I'm being pushed into a corner." The uneasiness she felt went beyond twinges to clutch at her stomach.

Just then the music stopped. "I found four glasses," said Margaret. "Let's break out some of my mom's booze."

"Your mom will know," objected Jackie.

"No, she won't. Here's a bottle that's half empty. She won't catch on if we take some."

Now the tightness in Jackie's stomach turned to cold fear. But somehow the glass was in her hand.

"Drink up, Jackie," said Bart. "Come on, we're waiting for you."

Jackie took a big gulp and choked. As the drink went down her throat, it burned.

"Take more," said Bart. "The more you drink, the better it tastes."

Jackie set down her glass, unwilling to try more. Her head felt strange. But Bart wanted to dance again. "Come on," he demanded.

Jackie dragged herself to her feet, not feeling like herself and hating the feeling. Bart's sweaty hands took hers, and his grip tightened. Jackie wanted to scream. "What shall I do?" she thought. "Mom was right. What shall I do?"

Desperately, she glanced at her watch. Ten after five. Suddenly she knew what to do. "I said I'd be home at 5:30. Gotta go," she said, picked up her coat and hurried out the door.

"Whew! I'll never try that again," she thought, grateful for the two blocks she had to walk in the cold fresh air. But Mom was waiting at the door.

"Where have you been, Jackie?"

"I told you this morning where I was going," answered Jackie. "Don't you remember I said I was going to Debbie's?"

Mom's gaze held steady. "Too bad you missed your cousins. Their school furnace broke down so they got a day off. Aunt Linda drove them over. They thought it'd be fun to see you."

In that moment Jackie felt like throwing up. Should she tell Mom the truth? Did Mom know anyway? All the hiding, the yucky feelings, the booze, the lies—all the telling herself it was okay when it wasn't. And she had missed her favorite cousins.

"Who am I lying to?" Jackie asked herself. "To my mom, or to myself?"

TO TALK ABOUT

▶In what way could Jackie's mother find out that Jackie wasn't at Debbie's?

▶What did Jackie mean when she asked, "Am I lying to my mom, or to myself?"

▶How does one lie lead to another? How did Jackie's choices keep getting her into deeper trouble?

▶What do you think might have happened to Jackie if she hadn't left when she did?

▶What are some of the possible dangers of hanging

around with much older kids?

▶When out with other kids, what is the value of having a set time for being home?

Do not let kindness and truth leave you. . . . Write them on the tablet of your heart. So you will find favor and good repute in the sight of God and man. (Proverbs 3:3-4, NASB)

Jesus, when I'm tempted to lie, give me the power of Your Holy Spirit to be truthful. Help me so my words and actions are honest before You and before other people. Thank You that when I'm honest I can like myself.

I'M SCARED, GOD

From the room below came the sound of voices. All his life Jeff had gone to bed hearing the low murmur. Yet these last weeks and months the voices held a different sound.

Quickly Jeff slipped out of bed and crept to the open stairway. Crouching on the wide floorboards of the old farmhouse, he peered down between the railing. At the dining room table sat Mom and Dad—Mom mending, Dad bending over a pile of papers.

As Jeff watched, Dad ran his fingers through his hair. "I don't know what to do, Karen. I've kept our expenses as low as I could. It's our best crop in twenty years. Yet we've never had a time like this. How can we make ends meet?"

172

Jeff's mom set down her mending, and circled the table. Leaning down, she hugged her husband. "I know, Nate. I know. We've talked about it so often."

Dad pushed back the papers. "I feel like a failure. No matter how hard I work, it isn't enough." His voice rose. "I'm afraid we'll lose the farm."

"Shhhhh, Nate." Gently Mom put her finger on his lips. "I don't want the children to hear."

Dad sighed. "If we lose the farm, they'll have to know."

"I don't blame you for being upset. I'm discouraged, too. And afraid. But at least we don't have a new house or new machinery to pay for. We've done everything we can to be careful."

As Jeff watched, tears came into his mother's eyes. This time it was Dad's turn to give a hug, and his voice changed. "I keep thinking of what Jesus said about the sparrows and the lilies. . . ."

As though she had memorized the words, Mom's voice joined his: "Look at the birds of the air; they do not sow or reap or store away in barns, and yet your heavenly Father feeds them."

She paused, as though forcing herself to go on. "If that is how God clothes the grass of the field, which is here today and tomorrow is thrown into the fire, will he not much more clothe you, O you of little faith?" (Matthew 6:26,30).

Mom's voice grew softer. "'O you of little faith?' I

173

never thought about it that way before. Jesus expects us to trust Him—to believe He'll take care of us." Her voice broke, but she went on. "No matter what happens, we'll be together."

Without making a sound, Jeff crept back to his room. For a long time he stood at the window, looking out under the light of the full moon. Nearby, from the branch of a large oak, hung the swing he'd used for as long as he could remember. Now he felt too old for it, but he wondered, "Will my little sister and brother grow up here enjoying that swing?"

Farther away, the brown stubs of corn stalks stretched out across a field. Seeing them, Jeff remembered the first time he'd driven the tractor—the planting, the growing, the harvesting. Dad tossing a golden ear of corn to see if he would catch it.

In that moment Jeff realized how much the farm meant to him. Down the road Tom's family had already lost their farm. And Gary's dad had lost his job at a farm equipment store. Was this how all of them had been feeling inside?

A worry knot formed and tightened in Jeff's chest. Returning to bed, he slid down beneath the quilt. "I'm scared, God," he began. "What if we. . . ?"

Then he remembered the verses he'd heard Mom and Dad talking about. He started his prayer over. "I'm scared, but You said You take care of every little bird. How do I stop worrying, Lord? How do I believe in You instead of being scared? Can You help me believe You're going to take care of us?"

TO TALK ABOUT

▶Do you think Jeff's family will lose the farm?

▶If they're forced to leave the farm, would that mean God didn't keep His promise to provide for them?

▶Does God take away all our problems just because we are Christians?

▶What are some things we might learn when our family faces big problems?

▶Do you know other verses Jeff could repeat to himself when he's afraid about the future?

▶Sometimes it's good to ask, "What if?" It helps us dream big dreams and set goals. Other times we make ourselves miserable by asking that question. Do you have a "what if?" that makes you afraid? If so, how can you start praying about it?

"Seek first his kingdom and his righteousness, and all these things will be given to you as well. Therefore do not worry about tomorrow, for tomorrow will worry about itself." (Matthew 6:33-34)

Jesus, when I'm scared, I let all the things that bother me go round and round in my head. Yet You know what I need. Help me believe in Your promises. Teach me to pray about things that worry me. If You take care of every little bird, You can take care of me.

RUN TO WIN

For the third time Kari checked her shoelaces to be sure they were tightly tied. Jumping up and down, she flexed every muscle. The spring sunshine warmed her face, yet she felt uneasy. "Can I run as well as I did when I had friends to cheer me on?" she wondered. "I miss them. It's hard being a new kid in this town."

She looked around the field, checking the long white lines someone had sprayed on the grass that morning. Everything was ready for the school track meet. Yet Kari's thoughts weren't on the 100-yard dash. She watched Mona, a classmate who would be running against her. "I wish I could laugh and feel sure about myself the way she does," thought Kari.

Two months before, after her family had prayed a good deal, Kari's dad bought the restaurant in town. He felt God wanted them to be here. Kari had to admit she thought so, too. It wasn't always fun, working together in the restaurant, but she liked the Christian music Dad played for background.

Even so, it had been difficult changing schools in February, and Kari wished her friends were here. "I want these kids to like me," she thought. "Being alone makes it much harder to be a Christian." Then she remembered one of the songs Dad had played the night before. Trying to work up her courage, she hummed softly to herself.

"Best of luck, Kari," said a voice, coming up behind her. "You'll do great."

Kari turned, and gratefulness welled up within her. It was just the encouragement she needed. "Thanks, Chad. Hope *you* do well."

A moment later Chad was at the starting line, and Kari cheered from the sideline. He stretched out, settled into his stride, and crossed the finish line. A roar went up from the spectators.

Now it was Kari's turn. With all her heart she wanted to win. "Maybe then I'd feel part of this town," she thought. Waiting at the starting line with Mona on her left, Kari prayed. "Help me, Lord. Help me."

An instant later she remembered the Scottish athlete Eric Liddell. By refusing to run on Sunday, he sacrificed an Olympic Gold Medal. Yet he won the Gold in a different event, then became a missionary to China.

Kari's prayer changed. "I want to honor You, Lord."

"On your mark!" shouted the starter. "Get set! Go!"

With a bound Kari was off. Like the wind she ran. Faster. Faster. Mona edged up. Out of the corner of her eye, Kari saw her, and put on more speed. Feeling as if her lungs would burst, she crossed the finish line. "Yaaaaaay, Kari!" came the cry. "Yaaaaaaay, Kari!" But it was a half-hearted cheer.

"Thank You, Jesus," she prayed silently. "Thanks for helping me win."

Her classmates gathered around her, offering congratulations. But Kari knew something was wrong. Soon most of them drifted over to where Mona was standing. Then Kari guessed their feelings. "It bothers them that I won. They've been together since kindergarten. They wanted Mona to be first."

Kari gathered up her jacket, and started to leave. The joy she had felt in winning started to sag, like the air leaking out of a bright balloon.

As she turned away, Kari bumped into two kids standing behind her.

"New in town, aren't you?" asked the girl.

"Right," answered Kari.

The boy next to her chimed in. "Your folks bought the restaurant, didn't they? You know, they really shouldn't play Christian music there. Some people won't like it. Hurt your business."

Kari's balloon of joy gave its final sputter of life. Her shoulders slumped. Where was Chad now? Where were the few others in this town who seemed to like her? With her whole heart she wanted these kids to like her, too.

Then another thought flashed through her mind. "Is this the real answer to my prayer? Where will I honor Jesus more—in winning the race, or in what I say to these kids?"

Kari straightened up, knowing she had to make a choice. For a moment she hesitated, wondering if the kids would laugh at her. Then she spoke. "Lots of people *do* like Christian music."

Inside, Kari knew she had won an even bigger race.

TO TALK ABOUT

▶Kari could have answered, "Oh, that's just my folks' choice of music. I don't have anything to do with it." What cost was there for Kari in answering the way she did? How do you think she felt inside?

▶Why did being new make it especially hard for Kari to stand up for her faith in Jesus?

▶How does our wish to be liked get in the way of giving an answer that honors Jesus?

▶God doesn't expect us to always win, but He calls us to be faithful to Him. What does it mean to be faithful?

▶How can the Holy Spirit help us? Can you think of a time when He helped you to honor Jesus?

I have fought the good fight. I have finished the race, I have kept the faith. (2 Timothy 4:7)

Jesus, it's hard to stand alone. With all my heart I want to be faithful to You. Give me the power of Your Holy Spirit and the courage I need. Thank You that even when I feel lonely, You're a friend who's always with me.

181

A FINAL
PROMISE

Well, how are you doing?

While reading this book, have you made any real-life choices? Have you discovered the secrets unlocked by your choice? Do they belong to you? If so, you might like to know something more.

When you make the choice you believe is best, you may struggle afterward. You might ask yourself, "Did I do the right thing?" Or, if kids give you a hard time, you could think, "Well, I made the best choice. But I'm not worth anything. Nobody cares about me." You feel miserable because you keep telling yourself you are worthless. Your feelings about yourself depend on the outward approval of those around you.

It's important to have approval from the right

people. Yet it's not worth having approval if it forces you to make wrong choices. Or feel sorry about good ones.

If you keep knocking yourself down, that can be harder to deal with than what other people say. God does just the opposite. When you make the best choice, the Holy Spirit supports you—if you let Him. He works in your good choices to help them become good habits. God also has special ways of showing that you are of value to Him.

Sometimes you know that right away. Other times it takes awhile. It may even be hard to see. When God honors us for being faithful to Him, it might not come in the way we think. *But it will come in God's best way!*

The Bible gives God's word for it—a promise that encouraged Olympic hero Eric Liddell. You, too, can claim that promise at a moment of choice: "Those who honor me I will honor" (1 Samuel 2:30).

May that secret also be yours.